Visa

Massoud Kermani

authorHOUSE®

AuthorHouse™ UK Ltd.
500 Avebury Boulevard
Central Milton Keynes, MK9 2BE
www.authorhouse.co.uk
Phone: 08001974150

First published by AuthorHouse   9/23/2010

ISBN: 978-1-4520-7578-5 (sc)

This book is printed on acid-free paper.

This book is written to commemorate the first anniversary of Iranian Presidential elections – June 2009

This novel is entirely a work of fiction. The names, characters and incidents portrayed in it, are the work of the author's imagination. Any resemblance to actual persons living or dead, events or localities is entirely coincidental.

This book is also published in Persian language

Can one tell the little sparrow not to flee, not to go?

When the skilled hunter flies near and low

Can you ask the little bird to stay?

When it's nest and younglings may soon fall prey,

Can you ask the nightingale not to fly?

It's free soul oppress and deny

Can you punish her for wanting to escape?

In whatever form, way or shape

The iron cage the cruel jailer has built

Must she stay and rot inside it and wilt?

The human soul too wants to be free

Free of oppression and suppression it wants to be

Can you ask a nightingale not to sing?

Shut it in a cage and clip it's tiny wings

Can you prevent a bird from nesting on the neighbour's tree?

Erect huge signs in the sky saying No entry

Can you place no entry signs in the sky?

And a birds entry into the neighbour's yard deny

Does a bird see borders from the sky when flying free and up high?

Massoud Kermani

A WORD FROM THE AUTHOR

I left Iran a few years before the Islamic Revolution and came to England to continue my education. Having completed my education, given family and work obligations and responsibilities I was unable to take-up any cultural activities.

The event that created a deep and unexpected transformation within my heart and soul and caused me to take-up writing once again and what stirred my subconscious into turmoil and activity were recent events that transpired in Iran.

The recent Iranian presidential election during which by accident I happened to be in Iran. The election during and prior, I personally witnessed the enthusiastic and whole hearted participation of the Iranian youth who wanted to have a say in their own future. Unfortunately however, as the world was to soon witness its aftermath, the elections results were stolen and the peoples vote discarded. The early disappointment soon turned into peaceful marches and demonstrations that were brutally and ruthlessly suppressed.

The green movement that represented hope and democracy and a better future was soon confronted by a wave of violence and brutal oppression and all the hopes and dreams of the younger generation were turned to dust.

The prisons were filled with authors, journalists, intellectuals and those who just happened to have been among those protestors who were arrested.

Another factor that contributed to my decision was the advice and encouragement of my dear cultured and talented friend, Mr. Majid Beheshti, who was able to inspire me to put pen to paper after a 31 year time lapse. I thank him from the bottom of my heart. I also thank my dearest wife, Deborah, for her great help in sub-editing this fictional play.

Characters in VISA

Name	Age	Name	Age
Arash	55	Amiri's Driver	25
Sarah	45	Qassem	25
Kian	17	Ghafur	38
Judge 1	50	Golnar	30
Judge 2 (Peter Jones)	65	Gardener	22
Home Office Barrister 1	45	Nargess	20
Home Office Barrister 2	45	Mustafa	30
Defence Barrister 1	40	Rafat	20
Defence Barrister 2	45	Rashid	28
Seyyed Mohsen	28	Barzan	65
Jeff	45	Robabeh	50
Sassan	45	Azam	25
Nazanine	35	Shams	20
Asgari	35	Nosrat	31
Fatemeh	37	Chinese Boy	12
Fereshteh	34	Chinese Man 1	25
Haj Agha Rostami	60	Chinese Man 2	30
Revolutionary Guard 1	25	Chinese Woman	30
Revolutionary Guard 2	26	First Worker	31
Nasser	45	Second Worker	40
Colonel Afshar	45	James	40
Maliheh	44	Court Stereographer	26
Sadeq	42	Hospital Receptionist	25
Shahin	45	Head Nurse	40
Hashem	30	Mother Sadigeh	82
Militia Police 1	18	Young Sassan	14
Militia Police 2	26	Haj Agha Salehi	45
Militia Police 3	21	Young Soldier	14
Nazanine Child	6	Café Owner	30
Hussein	26	Mammad Wolf	40
Abdullah	45	Mammad's Gang	
Saleh	37	Crowd in Hyde Park	
Bearded Man	24	Journalists in Court	
Colonel Amini	36		

ARASH'S HOUSE

7:00AM

A small ordinary house in London decorated in both Iranian and English styles. A few frames containing antique Iranian Miniatures depicting scenes from the Rubaiyat of Omar Khayam hang on the wall. A Persian carpet decorates the floor of the living room. A few picture frames containing old family photographs sit upon a small table. At the corner of the dining room, a 25 year old wedding picture of Sarah an English woman and Arash a tall and handsome Iranian man catches the eye. There are also pictures of their three children, Rosie 20, Keyvan 22 and Kian 17 showing them at various ages. A family photo showing the whole family posing together stands in the middle of the table. It is 7:00am. Sarah sets up breakfast. A few pieces of toast, some jam and some cheese are on the dining table. A few boxes of cereal, a bottle of milk and a few bowls are already set on the table.

SARAH: *Wearing casual clothes goes to the foot of the staircase and calls in a loud voice*

"Breakfast is ready."

ARASH: *"I can't find my blue neck tie."*

SARAH: *"It's down here. I just got it back from the cleaners."*

Arash walks down the stairs wearing a suit, his shirt collar open, he is cleanly shaven but seems rather tired and irritable. He sits in the chair at the head of the dining table.

ARASH: *"May I have a cup of tea?"*

Sarah places a mug in front of him.

1

SARAH: *"Here you are dear."* With a smile

"Early this morning Kian put his jogging suit on and went for a jog. It's really good for youth his age to be interested in sports and exercise."

ARASH: *"In a few years, once he is older he will say farewell to sports, then all he will think and care about will be girls. Just like his brother Keyvan."*

SARAH: *"I wish that he would also care about his studies as Keyvan does so that he can get into a good school. By the way love, I don't think I mentioned this, it is going to be a busy weekend. Keyvan and Rosie are planning to have some of their friends over. It is supposed to be very nice and sunny. What do you say to a barbeque?"*

ARASH: *"That is fine with me."* After a small pause

"By the way love, what time do I have to be in court this morning?"

SARAH: *"9:30am, courtroom number four."*

Sarah looks at the clock.

"You don't have much time dear."

There is silence, Arash looks a bit anxious.

SARAH: *"What's wrong Arash? Why aren't you eating your breakfast?"*

ARASH: *"I don't know for which asylum seeker I am supposed to be interpreting today."*

Sarah looks at him with a curious smile.

"Sometimes I have to translate some statements so ridiculous and relate some claims that are so baseless that I become totally embarrassed. I know, and the judge very well knows and probably everybody in the courtroom knows, that the statements that some of these asylum seekers make are such nonsense and a load of baseless lies. But, well, regardless a series of legal routines have to be observed as a matter of course before any judgements may be handed down."

Sarah listens with interest.

"Some fellow, named Saeed, just last week was claiming that he was gay.

2

He named a few partners too! Claiming that he had had homosexual relationships with these people. Then the fellow turns to me and asks, shall I name so and so also? I tell him my dear man, what on earth are you asking me for? Was I there with you when you and him.....well, you know!? You just go ahead and say whatever you want to say and I will translate for you and relate it to the court word for word. I am not your advisor. Do not say anything that you do not wish me to translate. All this fellow had to show for his claims were a handful of made-up names that he mentioned and that's just about all. Now I am left to explain in full detail all the rubbish that this chap just uttered to Her Majesty's court! Sometimes I think that the judge might think that I am making all this up as I go along and might be in the same camp as these people."

Both Sarah and Arash laugh.

"Maybe I am just getting too good at this job."

They both laugh.

"The fellow tells the judge that should the court refuse him asylum and deport him back to Iran, he will be shot the minute he steps off the plane since he is gay. Later it was found out that this guy is married with four children. I bet if the court did grant him a VISA he would try and bring most of his relatives to this country, then when he gets his British Passport he would go back to Iran for a holiday at every opportunity he gets. I've seen it all before sweetheart."

SARAH: *"Surely they can't all be this way?"*

ARASH: *"Of course not dear."*

After a pause

"Some of them especially those seeking political asylum are very well educated people, well known too, some are authors, journalists, well recognized writers and university professors, human rights activists, artists etc. These types of asylum seekers are usually fully documented and able to show legitimate proof. The Home Office very quickly honours their requests."

"Almost all of them are successfully granted permanent residence. This

leaves those who are unknowns and who have nothing to back up their claims or documents that will show that asylum laws apply to their case. In these cases, the Home Office rejects their claims and they are deported. Some of these people turn to the appeals court. Most don't speak a word of English. That is where I come in and this is what has become my livelihood, when I take over the interpretation and translation of their appeals claims."

SARAH: *"I see. I understand now. I thought all these people will be granted asylum from the court."*

ARASH: *"No. That is not exactly how it works. Only those who are denied from the Home Office apply to the court."*

Arash pauses for a moment

"The translation work is the easy part. But dealing with these people is not easy. The solicitor asks a question. The fellow, instead of answering the question, replies with another question. Or, for instance the solicitor asks the fellow 'How did you manage to enter the United Kingdom?' Instead of answering the question he goes on about how he had to trek through the mountains into Turkey and all the suffering he had to endure! I tell him, dear man just answer the question you were asked.....he tells me what's it to you? You just translate whatever I say. Then when the judge rejects his appeal, he blames me and goes on a rant on how I failed him and didn't translate what he had to say properly. This is what I do my dear. It is a daily war of nerves. There really is no satisfaction in this work."

Kian enters the house panting. He is wearing shorts and a t-shirt, jogging shoes and socks up to his knees. Sarah and Arash both fall silent.

KIAN: *"I ran around the park for almost an hour and a half."*

He drops into a chair next to Arash.

ARASH: *"No kidding. That's a new one. Well done. Well done."*

Looks Kian over with a satisfied grin on his face.

KIAN: *"Baba (Dad), remember that you promised to get me a very good laptop today with a lot of memory. You gave your word. You haven't forgotten have you?"*

4

ARASH: *"Alright, sure, I haven't forgotten."*

KIAN: *"Can I get some orange juice mum?"*

SARAH: *"Why don't you have a shower first?"*

Kian goes upstairs.

SARAH: *"Translating is your profession. It's a job you need to do. You shouldn't let your emotions interfere with your work. In any case, these people all obviously had a reason to bring all these hardships upon themselves and abandon their homes and countries. It should not make a difference, whether their motives were political or economical. Your job is to present to the court their reasons as they see them and express them and nothing more. Is it not so? And if they hold you responsible and give you any rubbish, you should really ignore it all. Don't make life difficult for yourself and us, remember Arash, all that we rely on for our livelihood is the salary you bring home. What are you on about being emotionally hurt and all that? What's wrong with you today? We are definitely not in a situation where you can resign.*

"You very well know that if I were in the same shape as ten years ago, when I were young and fit with the educational background that I have, I would get a decent job for myself. But nowadays, with every couple of hours that I spend on my feet, I would have to lie down on the bed or the sofa for at least ten minutes. My heart aches and I become short of breath. In this situation....."

ARASH: *Cuts Sarah off*

"Who said anything about resigning? I was just letting off some steam. I know how you feel physically. I prefer that you stay home and take care of things here and get as much rest as you need. You are the heart of this family, I never want anything to happen to you, god forbid."

Turns to Sarah

"By the way, did you have your medicine today?"

SARAH: *Hands Arash his tie*

"No, not yet, I will take it later."

Looks at her watch.

"It is getting late, you better leave before traffic gets heavy."

Sarah begins to clear the dining table and Arash puts on his tie as he looks into the mirror hanging on the wall.

ARASH*: As he is leaving the house*

"Well dear, I am on my way. Is there anything you need?"

Sarah goes to the front door.

SARAH*: "Take care love. I will see you later. Bye"*

A STREET IN LONDON

8:00AM

Arash is walking toward the bus stop through the usual hustle and bustle of everyday life. Arash's thoughts can be heard.

ARASH: *"It's ten years since I started to be a court translator for Iranian and Afghan refugees. Six, seven years back they only needed me part time, now however with the increasing volume of asylum seekers, it has become more than a full-time occupation. I have translated in so many different courtrooms in London now that most judges, solicitors and even doormen in these courts know me on a first name basis and recognise me. The pay isn't so bad either. It's a living wage. I get by. My work isn't physical. But there is mental stress involved. This is really tiring. It takes a lot out of you. Sometimes it makes one go almost berserk just to think what hell they are willing to put themselves through for a British visa. During the Shah's rule, a couple of years before he was toppled, I came to England as a student. At the time I did not know a single Iranian national seeking asylum in this country. If I were to write about the turmoil and uncertainties these souls go through, I would need to fill a hundred volumes or more."*

"Some of them are quite brave souls and on the other hand some are quite stupid. A case in point is a fellow called Seyyed Mohsen Razavi from the city of Hamedan. He had asked for asylum basing his case on two precedents. Firstly that he had converted into Zoroastrianism from Islam and secondly that he had been politically active against the Islamic Republic. He claimed that should he be returned to Iran, he would be considered an apostate and shot twice, once for being an apostate and once for being a political activist against the regime. His motives for

7

presenting two reasons to ensure him the asylum he was seeking were that in-case the first one was not enough to ensure approval, the second would kick in as a fail-safe mechanism and guarantee him the result. May god have mercy upon us all!!!"

THE COURT

A judge wearing a white wig is sitting upon his high backed chair. The Barrister for the defence and the Barrister representing the Home Office are also wearing wigs. Arash is standing next to Seyyed Mohsen, a young bearded 28 year old man with a presentable demeanour.

HOME OFFICE BARRISTER: *Turns to Arash*

"Would you ask him to state his full name please?"

ARASH*: In Persian*

"Tell the court your full name?"

MOHSEN*: "My full name is Seyyed Mohsen Razavi."*

Arash repeats the name and Mohsen nods in agreement.

HOME OFFICE BARRISTER*:*

"Then you are really a Seyyed?"

Turns to judge

The term Seyyed refers to those who are or claim that they are descendents "of the children of the prophet of Islam."

Home Office Barrister turns to Mohsen

"If you are a Seyyed, from which Imam (Saint) are you a descendent of?"

Arash translates

MOHSEN*: "My ancestor is the 8th Imam of Shiite Islam, Imam Reza, God bless him."*

Arash translates.

HOME OFFICE BARRISTER*: Turns to Mohsen and stares him directly in* *the eyes.*

"What kind of a personage was Imam Reza? How would you describe him? Please explain him fully?"

Arash translates in an elaborate manner.

MOHSEN: *Ponders the question for a while.*

"Ask him why he is asking me this?"

ARASH: *Leans towards Mohsen*

"I already told you, you are not allowed to ask the barrister any questions, you are here to answer them."

MOHSEN: *"As long as I don't understand the reason he has behind this kind of questioning, I won't answer a damn thing. You go ahead and translate that for him."*

Arash translates with a frustrated look on his face.

HOME OFFICE BARRISTER: *As he turns to the judge*

"I insist that the gentleman answers the question your honour."

MOHSEN'S BARRISTER: *To the judge*

"I object to this question your honour!"

THE JUDGE: *To Mohsen's barrister*

"The objection is overruled. Please advise your client that he must answer the question."

MOHSEN: *"I am the one who has decided to change my religion. Imam Reza, God forbid is not the one who wants to convert. What does this whole business have to do with Imam Reza? His blessed holiness did not direct me to convert. Regardless, why are you trying to drag his holiness into this? God forbid, is Imam Reza the cause of the Iranian people's misery? Translate what I said word for word."*

Arash pauses before he relates Mohsen's tirade.

HOME OFFICE BARRISTER: *To Arash "What did he say? "*

Arash translates.

THE JUDGE: Angrily *"Don't you realize that you are in a courtroom? You were asked to describe Imam Reza's personality. What is your opinion about your ancestor? Answer the question and no more."*

ARASH: *Turns to Mohsen and relates the judge's words*

"If you don't answer, it will hurt your case."

MOHSEN: *Takes a sip of water*

"His holiness Imam Reza was a true saint. He would heal the deaf, the blind and the crippled. Hundreds of thousands of pilgrims come to his tomb every year, in the holy city of Mashad."

HOME OFFICE BARRISTER: *To Mohsen*

"Do you believe that Imam Reza can heal the deaf and the blind, the crippled and the sick?"

Arash translates.

MOHSEN: *"Of course I believe this, I have personally witnessed it. I was there when a camel escaped from the slaughter house, and managed to get to Imam's holy tomb through all the crazy traffic of the city and squatted right in the middle of the mosque's court yard and begged the Imam for mercy, which was duly granted. The butchers who were chasing it decided to forgo the slaughter and the camel was set free. Two days later someone who was blind at child birth was healed and could see again. The crowd who witnessed this miracle gathered around the man and began to tear his clothes apart to carry home as holy relics, as if they had gotten hold of the shroud of Turin."*

HOME OFFICE BARRISTER: *To the judge*

"I have no more questions on this subject, your honour."

Arash translates

HOME OFFICE BARRISTER: *"Your claim was that you were politically active against the Islamic Republic of Iran. Is this true? Just answer yes or no!"*

Arash translates. "Just say yes or no."

MOHSEN: *"Yes, let me explain and expand on this issue in full."*

Arash translates.

HOME OFFICE BARRISTER: *"No thank you, it is not at all necessary. All this is reflected in full detail in your file. However, I have this question for you. If you would please turn to the judge and answer. Who is the present speaker of the parliament of the Islamic Republic of Iran?"*

Arash translates.

MOHSEN: *Ponders a while "Mr. Hashemi Rafsanjani"*

Turns to Arash and asks in a desperate tone

"Am I right? Come on man, we are both Iranians, help me out here! If you know for sure tell him the right answer."

ARASH: *"He is asking you, not me" Turns to the judge. "Hashemi Rafsanjani"*

HOME OFFICE BARRISTER: *Shakes his head sarcastically in disagreement*

"Wrong answer. Name four of the ministers of the present cabinet of the Islamic government of Iran?"

MOHSEN: *Seems confused and is muttering something to himself*

"I don't remember" to Arash "tell them a few names yourself."

ARASH: *"I am not allowed."*

HOME OFFICE BARRISTER: *Looking at Mohsen angrily*

"You don't even know the names of any of the heads of this regime. Against whom were you politically objecting, may I ask?"

Arash elaborately translates to Mohsen.

MOHSEN: *"I was fighting against those cruel Mullahs who have taken*

hope away from the hearts of the people of Iran and who have forced the country's young to flee in desperation. In Iran there is no work for us, no opportunities, no hope."

HOME OFFICE BARRISTER: *"Very well then, since you were fighting against the Mullah's, name four of the Friday prayer leaders in Iran."*

Arash translates. Mohsen quietly mutters a few names to himself but seems uncertain, he stays silent.

HOME OFFICE BARRISTER: *Turns and addresses the judge*

"It is clearly evident your honour that every claim this defendant has made in this court room is baseless and false. I therefore move to deny the claimant's request for political asylum and ask that he be deported from this country forthwith."

Arash translates. The judge looks at the file in front of him and the defence barrister stands up to speak.

MOHSEN: *Turns to Arash and says in an angry and disturbed tone*

"Yeah, sure all that I have said are lies, and all that these people say is true, translate that for the judge."

Arash translates with a bewildered look on his face.

THE JUDGE: *To Mohsen*

"Stay silent"

ARASH: *To Mohsen*

"The judge has not allowed you to speak. Stay quiet."

MOHSEN: *To Arash*

"You never mind, just translate."

Mohsen goes on in a whimpering tone

"Mr judge, what? Do you think I was sick in the head to tie myself under

the belly of a juggernaut and travel three hundred kilometres and 2 days on an empty stomach to get here from France, believe me, the heat from that truck's exhaust seared half my body. I was almost barbequed."

Arash rapidly translates as the Home Office barrister and the judge listen intently.

"You can see for yourself, I am not lying."

"If I had hope, if I had a decent livelihood in my country, if I had a future would I put myself through this misery? You be the judge."

The judge indicates to the courtroom guards, they quickly approach

Mohsen and take him away.

ON THE STREET

Arash walks towards the bus stop, Arash's thoughts can be heard.

ARASH*: "They all share the illusion that once they manage to reach this island of hope and glory a red carpet reception awaits them and the prime minister, Mr. Gordon Brown, will personally take time out of his busy schedule to welcome them and grant them asylum and permanent residence with full and complete benefits that this entails. They think it's that simple."*

Arash reaches the bus stop and gets on the bus.

THE COURT HOUSE LOBBY

9:30AM

After a routine body search and the exchange of the usual pleasantries with the now very familiar faces, Arash enters the courthouse. Jeff, a forty year old clerk in a neatly pressed suit approaches Arash carrying a file in his right hand."

JEFF: *"Morning Arash! You are early today."*

ARASH: *"The traffic was light and the bus was early."*

JEFF: *"The court will go into session an hour and a half later than usual today."*

He continues as he hands Arash a file.

"Could you manage to translate for an Afghan national? I am not quite sure whether he speaks Pashtoo or Farsi?"

Then he glances into the file and closes it.

"Oh, O.K. he is a Farsi speaker."

ARASH: *"As long as he doesn't speak with a strong Afghan accent, I can manage it. What time is he scheduled for?"*

Jeff looks at the file again.

JEFF: *"It is either on Thursday or Friday, once I know for certain I shall let your wife know by telephone. By the way, I wouldn't worry about his accent, since he spent a few years in Iran as a migrant worker."*

ARASH: *"Not a problem. We will be waiting for your call."*

JEFF: *"I will give you a shout for today's case in about one and a half hours from now. It will be held in courtroom number 4. See you in a bit."*

Jeff walks away and Arash wanders around the very nearly empty hallways of the courthouse. After getting a cup of coffee from the vending machine he takes a seat on one of the benches along the hallway. He opens his briefcase and takes out a file and an English newspaper. He starts to read as he drinks his coffee. At the same moment an Iranian couple attract his attention. The woman is Nazanine Afshar, a 35 year old with long black hair wearing a blouse and a modest skirt over black tights. The husband is Sassan Yazdani, around 45 years old wearing a grey suit, white shirt and black moccasins. In the middle of some sort of discussion they approach Arash and sit on the bench immediately behind him. They take a quick glance at Arash who seems quite affixed to his English newspaper.

NAZANINE: *Seems worried and anxious*

"I wish they won't bombard us with all those damn questions again."

SASSAN: *Trying to calm Nazanine down*

"Don't worry so much, it will be all right. But remember what the translator told us, this is the final appeals court that will issue the final judgement."

Takes a few sheets of paper out of his pocket, unfolds them and hands them to Nazanine.

"Carefully look at these and study and memorise them. Remember what we practised last night."

NAZANINE: *As she looks at the notes*

"They say it is going to be very difficult, I am very nervous."

SASSAN: *Cuts her off*

"Do you want to be granted asylum or not?"

Nazanine stays silent.

"Now is not the time for this. We chose this path out of desperation and we have no choice but to stick it through to the very end. Of course it is hard. I fully understand you and how you feel, it is just as hard for me to

go in front of the judge, the barristers and this translator guy and confess to all that I have to confess to. Believe me, it is not easy for me either to have to utter all these words and sentences in front of these people. I am as tired of this rubbish as you are."

He takes a few more sheets out of his jacket's pocket, looks at Nazanine.

"I am going to read you my prepared statement, see what you think."

NAZANINE: *Nods her head as she looks at her own notes.*

SASSAN: *"Your honour, please allow me to say to you that while in Iran my main occupation was being a school teacher. I used to teach Persian at Shahid Ghateh elementary school. On that sordid day at 1:30pm I was dictating to the children."*

THE CLASSROOM AT SHAHID GHATEH ELEMENTARY

2.00 PM

In the classroom the children sit on their benches and listen to Sassan the Farsi language teacher as he slowly reads from the text book and dictates to them. Mr. Asgari knocks on the classroom door and enters.

ASGARI: *"You have a phone call from Ms. Fatemeh Rostami."*

SASSAN: *Approaches Mr Asgari*

"Please tell her that I am busy right now teaching class, I will call her back later."

ASGARI: *"I swear I already told her, again and again that you are in class and do not like to be disturbed, but she is very insistent. She says that she won't hang up until she speaks to you."*

Sassan accompanies Mr. Asgari out of the classroom.

"By the way, Haj Agha Rostami also called for you twice today."

SASSAN: *"Haj Agha Rostami! The Friday prayer leader of Bardsir? Are you sure?"*

ASGARI: *"Yes, but I didn't know anything about him being the Friday prayer leader of Bardsir, this is the first time I spoke to him. He seemed really pissed off, he was really rude to me. First he insisted that he must speak to you. When I told him that it is not possible since you were in class he got very angry and called me a few unmentionable names. I told him that I was the assistant principle of this school and not the janitor for*

19

him to have run around like an errand boy and that he should watch the way he speaks to me. He drew on his treasury of unmentionables once again and I immediately hung up."

SASSAN: *In a worried and anxious tone*

"You shouldn't have hung up on him. Haj Agha Rostami is Fatemeh Rostami's father as well as the chief Shariaa judge. Don't you know who he is? He is a very tough, cruel and ruthless judge. He has already condemned several poor and destitute souls to be hanged or stoned to death. He makes a point of throwing the first and the last stones himself. He thinks this will be spiritually rewarding in the hereafter."

ASGARI: *Seems petrified*

"May all the saints have mercy upon my soul. Mr Yazdani, I am on my hands and knees, please tell me what to do?"

They pass through a narrow hallway

"God forbid, do you think I am in trouble with Haj Agha Rostami? For God sake when you talk to his daughter please tell her that Asgari is at your service, tell her that I didn't realize whom I was speaking to."

SASSAN: *As they approach the office*

"Don't worry. Let me first find out what she wants from me in such a rush."

NASSER LOTFI AND MS. FATEMEH'S LIVING ROOM

WEDNESDAY 2:00PM

Fatemeh and her cousin Fereshteh are sitting in the living room. They both have long dark hair, slight make-up on and wearing the traditional modest longcoat. They both appear to be around 35ish. The living room is a large space, a hand-made Persian rug covers the floor. Expensive furniture is spread around the room. A few expensive paintings hang on the walls. On a small table stands the picture of two seven or eight year old kids.

Fereshteh is chain smoking and pacing about the room. She appears distressed.

Fatemeh holding the phone to her ear and impatiently waiting to speak to Sassan.

FATEMEH: *"Don't worry so much, you will have a heart attack, and put out that dammed cigarette, you are pregnant for god sake, it's not good for the baby. You shouldn't be smoking so much. Rest assured, we will take care of them. My father has already taken the initiative. I promise you he will make them pay with their worthless lives."*

FERESHTEH: *While sobbing loudly*

"How could Shahin do this to me? I am three months pregnant with his child. I am nurturing the fruit of his loins in my womb"

Says loudly. "Oh my dear Lord, please help me, what suffering I am going through. What am I going to do with this whore Nazanine. No wonder we always couldn't stand this witch. You could tell what a whore she is from

21

a mileaway."

FATEMEH: *"Do you think it least matters to this pimping bastard, Yazdani, or this whore if they destroy our lives for a measly couple of million Tomans. Well I tell you, they have got it wrong."*

Fereshteh is holding her face and sobbing desperately.

"I told you that they deceived Nasser and Shahin, they seduced them. All for money, the debts they owed them. You should have seen how Nazanine would flirt with Nasser and how she would try to seduce him. She is an evil enchantress."

THE OFFICE AT SHAHID GHATEH ELEMENTARY

WEDNESDAY 2:00PM

The office at Shahid Ghateh is a room about 3½ by 4 metres long. A few desks and file cabinets can be seen against the wall. A telephone sits on the desk. The handset is off and placed on the desk. Sassan enters the office and goes straight towards the telephone and picks it up. He begins to speak to Fatemeh who is impatiently waiting on the end of the line. Asgari leaves and closes the door behind him. Sassan is left alone in the room.

SASSAN: *"Hello Ms. Fatemeh, I hope nothing untoward or unpleasant has happened for you to feel it necessary to drag me out of a classroom during a lesson."*

FATEMEH: *While screaming into the phone*

"Hello my foot, you shameless bastard! What do you teach those innocent kids over there? Lessons in shamelessness? Promiscuity?"

SASSAN: *He is shocked*

"Madam, what on earth are you talking about? What are you saying? What is going on? What have I done for you to find yourself justified to address me in this rude manner?"

FATEMEH: *"Where the hell were you last Sunday at 3:30pm in the afternoon?"*

SASSAN: *"I was teaching a class right here at this school. You can come and ask the principle yourself if you don't believe me. Why are you asking anyway?"*

FATEMEH: *"Where was Nasser? Huh? Answer me?"*

SASSAN: *Seems very nervous*

"Nasser your husband?"

He pauses.

"How the hell should I know where he was? Am I supposed to be your husband's chaperone? Maybe he had gone home?"

FATEMEH: *"What home? Huh? He certainly wasn't at his home, you shameless bastard. You piece of shit. He was at your home, with your dear lovely Nazanine. You pandering pimp."*

SASSAN: *"This is absolutely unthinkable, impossible. My dear lady you shouldn't believe all the rubbish that you are told. You shouldn't accuse people of such ugly and dreadful acts. Have you no shame lady? Have you gone mad? This is an abomination."*

FATEMEH: *"You shameless little man, I saw my husband enter your house with my own two eyes. Where is Mr. Shahin Sedeqat right now? Answer me you bloody bastard."*

SASSAN: *"I saw Shahin at the foreign exchange place at 8 o'clock this morning, he was with Nasser, your husband. I had gone there to clear my debt with him. Immediately after that I returned to school to attend my class.....because I am administering an exam today and that is the God honest truth. I have no idea where they are or where they have been ever since. As God is my witness, out of the deep respect that I hold for Haj Agha Rostami, I am holding myself back and stomaching what you just said and trying very hard to continue to address you with respect. Ms Fatemeh, if you are so concerned about him, why don't you inquire from his wife, Ms. Fereshteh, your own cousin?"*

FATEMEH: *"Fereshteh and I are fully aware of all your hanky panky. You and your whore of a wife, that bitch Nazanine, have an enterprise going. You are taking our husbands for a ride and cleaning up. You throw your whore wife into their arms to work off your debts. You and your morally bankrupt wife are corrupting our innocent husbands. You should be ashamed of yourself. You shameless pimping piece of shit. Is this how you return all the kindness that Fereshteh and I have shown you? I told everything to my dear father. He has promised to seek out our vengeance.*

He is going to take good care of you! You must remember how my father ordered the stoning to death of that harlot in Bardsir. That is exactly what is going to happen to you and your whore of a wife."

Sassan looks pale, finds it hard to speak, he drops the phone, steps back and runs into the chair located just behind him and falls on to the office floor. Mr. Asgari hurriedly enters the room.

ASGARI: *"Are you all right Mr. Yazdani? What is going on? What happened?"*

He helps Sassan off the floor and into a chair. Sassan is dizzy and disorientated, he doesn't answer.

"You seem very pale. Let me bring you a glass of water."

Sassan gets off the chair and without saying a word dashes out of the room. Asgari follows for a small distance and shouts after him.

"Mr. Yazdani, where are you going in such a hurry? What's happened? Wait till you feel a bit better. May God help us all."

NASSER LOTFI AND MS. FATEMEH'S HOUSE

DININGROOM

FATEMEH: *As she turns off her mobile*

"He talks as if he hasn't got a clue. Well I gave him a good piece of my mind."

Turns to Fereshteh.

"I must inform father immediately. He is waiting for my phone call right now."

She dials a number on the phone, waits a little while....then excitedly....

"Hello father...... as you has directed I told everything to Yazdani.......... yes....yes..... He denied everything......yes. Then he dropped the phone and left...... Fereshteh isn't feeling so well either. I am afraid that she might have a miscarriage......ok alright. Well I have to go, goodbye."

As she replaces the handset she turns to Fereshteh.

"Father said he personally has everything under control. Don't you worry."

ON THE STREET TO SASSAN YAZDANI'S APARTMENT

WEDNESDAY – 2:30PM

Sassan is walking on the pavement. He is lost deep in his thoughts. After passing a couple of blocks, he stops in front of an eight story building. He opens the front door and quickly starts to climb the stairs, he stops in front of one of the apartments, and he pauses slightly, then reaches into his pocket and takes out a key. He slowly opens the door to the apartment. He notices the metal tipped pointed shoes that Shahin Sedeqat usually wears immediately inside the door of the apartment. At the end of the hallway, he sees Sedeqat's brown leather jacket hanging on the clothes rack. After a bit of contemplation he closes the door and leaves.

IN THE PARK

WEDNESDAY AROUND 3 P.M.

The sun is going down and the park seems deserted. Sassan, lost deep in thought walks aimlessly around the park. He sits on a bench placed beneath an old Oak tree in an isolated corner. His empty stare is fixed upon a group of young boys playing football in the distance. Meanwhile, Haj Agha Rostami, a fat cleric with a full beard, black turban and wearing a light brown robe approaches as if he had been following and watching Sassan for a while. He sits on a bench right opposite Sassan. Sassan suddenly notices the unexpected visitor and springs to his feet in terror. Two revolutionary guards who are accompanying Haj Agha Rostami watchfully stand nearby. Sassan is speechless.

ROSTAMI: *With a dirty grin*

"Good morning and god's blessings dear Mr. Yazdani. How do you do this beautiful day?"

SASSAN: *He tries to get a hold of himself*

"Good morning your holiness… I didn't at all notice your Excellencies presence Haj Agha Rostami. Please forgive me."

ROSTAMI: *"Please Mr. Yazdani, not at all, would you sit down?"*

Sassan hesitantly sits back on the bench

"Well we didn't have the pleasure of visiting you at the school, it is fortunate to have run into you at the Park."

Sassan's petrified gaze is fixed upon the two revolutionary guards who accompanied Rostami, Rostami who notices Sassan's apprehension says with a smile.

"What is it Mr. Yazdani you seem rather disturbed, worried perhaps?"

Sassan is still staring at the two guards who are waiting nearby.

"I hope the presence of the brothers is not bothering you?!"

Continues with a sarcastic grin.

"There is no problem, if you wish I could ask them to leave us alone."

With a gesture the two guards begin to walk away.

"Is that better?"

He looks at Sassan.

"Now we may have a heart to heart without any apprehensiveness and in more privacy, don't you agree?"

Rostami looks at the two guards who are now quite a distance away.

"It is for these selfless revolutionary guards that our muslim nation enjoys this security, comfort and serenity that the dear lord has blessed us with. Just imagine what would befall this innocent nation if it were not for the brave and selfless efforts of these young men whom ceaselessly uphold the law of our land? If it wasn't for Judges like me and these upholders of the law what you would be looking at right now is (he points to the youth playing football in the park) some sick pervert committing acts of soddemy with people's children under the shade of these trees! Had the dear lord not descended through his good prophet the blessed punishment of lapidation for such acts you would be seeing whores and whore mongers fornicating each other all over this park like dogs."

"It is for these heavenly laws that we do not have to witness these ungodly scenes in our streets, alleys and bazaars."

Sassan is looking at the ground with his head down.

"Let's take a stroll around the park, shall we?"

Sassan looks at him with suspicion and hesitation.

"Come on get up!"

Sassan gets off the bench and they start to walk.

"Mr Yazdani, the dear lord has bestowed the superior holy class with ultimate wisdom. Sharia judges like me are like gardeners who are duty bound to identify useless weeds that grow amongst the flowers and uproot them so that the useful plants can thrive. Just look (he points to a garden full of beautiful flowers) this is a case in point. You cannot see one nasty weed amongst these flowers. There couldn't be. Otherwise these flowers and shrubs wouldn't be so lovely and alive. The holy clergy and judges are like shepherds whose duty it is to tend the flock. If one or two sheep among the flock come down with communicable disease we identify them and quickly destroy them."

There is silence, they approach a roundabout.

"Mr Yazdani! I am afraid that I must say that you and your wife are diseased, you are infected with a dangerous and contagious disease, a kind of black plague for which there is no cure. You have endangered marital convention in our Islamic society with your ugly and corrupt behaviour. Corruption has taken root in your heart and soul like a dreaded cancer and turned you into a walking cancerous tumour."

Rostami draws a small circle on the ground in the middle of the roundabout using his cane.

"Two holes should be dug for you and your wife in the middle of this round-about, about this diameter and one and a half metres deep."

He looks at Sassan as if sizing him up for the hole, Sassan looks scared.

"Mr Yazdani, my dear daughter Fatimeh criticises me for not being as tough as I should be in upholding Sharia laws of retaliation and stoning to death. She told me that the injustice that you and your wife will have brought upon her family is going to end up in destroying her marriage. She has asked me to do something about it. I said my dear daughter one must not rush things when it comes to matters upholding justice. First one must create a case file reflecting all the corrupt and unspeakable acts that have been committed and then refer this to the good lord's court of Islamic justice."

SASSAN: *Shaking in his boots.* *"I do not quite understand what you mean Haj Agha!"*

ROSTAMI: *"Don't you remember the glorious rites that we held in public in Bardsir a couple of years ago?"* *Sassan stays silent – Rostami continues- now shouting.*

"I am referring to the stoning of that harlot, Yazdani. You stupid man, you seem to have lost your memory?"

SASSAN: *"I didn't have the honour of witnessing those rites. I got sick at the onset and passed out."*

ROSTAMI: *Laughing*

"God willing you will not even get a chance to pass out during the stoning that will be arranged for you. You shall be able to take part from the beginning to the end. Then you and your wife will leave this world like two whining dogs." *Sassan is absolutely petrified. He steps back – Rostami follows him.* *"You are exactly like those weeds that grow amongst the flowers. You must be uprooted."*

Sassan is stunned and terrified; he takes a few steps back and then runs away.

WAITING ROOM IN THE COURTHOUSE

Arash is sitting with his back to Sassan and Nazanine pretending to be reading his newspaper, but he is actually listening to their conversation with curiosity.

SASSAN: *"OK, stand before me and pretend that you are in the courtroom. Before the courtroom gets crowded lets practice the first part, and act with feeling just as if you are addressing the judge."*

NAZANINE: *"Your honour, when Sassan and I got married, we did not have enough money to rent an apartment of our own and had to stay and live with Sassan's brother and sister in a small three bedroom apartment in the Nasiabad area of Tehran. Life was very hard for us in that little apartment. After living there for about a year, my husband Sassan borrowed one million Tomans each from Mr Nassir Lotfi and Mr Shahin Sedaqet who own an exchange bureau on Shahid Dadbin Street. We managed to rent a small apartment near my mother in-laws. He gave them post-dated cheques."*

A DESERTED STREET IN THE NASIABAD NEIGHBOURHOOD OF TEHRAN

SATURDAY 8.30 A.M.

Nazanine is wearing a brown headscarf a dark coloured light weight coat and black trousers. She is pacing along the side of the street as if awaiting a taxi. Immediately as she notices Nasser Lotfi, a bearded man who seems in his mid forties, she walks toward him.

NAZANINE: *"Good morning Mr. Lotfi"*

NASSER: *He looks at well dressed and very nicely made-up Nazanine and is slightly taken aback.*

"Hello Ms. Nazanine! What brings you to this neck of the woods?"

NAZANINE: *"To be honest, I wanted to see you before you got to the Exchange Bureau."*

NASSER: *With an open smile.*

"I am always happy to see you."

NAZANINE: *"Mr Lotfi, I wanted to speak to you regarding the money we owe you."*

NASSER: *"Ms Nazanine, it wouldn't look right if we talk to each other on the street, specially about money and debts."*

He pauses for a moment

"Why don't we step inside the café across the street and talk about your debt over there?"

NAZANINE: *Looks at her wrist watch   "I don't have much time I have to be at work at the hospital on time.*

She pauses for a moment

"OK then I'll try not to take much of your time."

They walk across the street and enter the coffee shop.

THE COFFEE SHOP

Nazanine is sitting opposite Nasser. There are two cups of tea on the table. Nasser lights a cigarette and takes a deep draw.

NAZANINE: *"You are well aware that Haj Fatimeh, and Fereshteh, and I do not get along very well. It has been quite a while since they have broken up with me, they do not even talk to me. That is why I decided to come and talk to you about our debt personally. God is my witness, Sassan hasn't a clue that I am here, otherwise he would never have allowed me to come."*

Nasser listens as he sips his tea.

"As you are aware, every day after Sassan comes home from school he takes a small break and then works with his taxi till late at night. Believe me, sometimes he doesn't get home until 2.00 am. You know that he is of feeble health and suffers from stomach ulcers. As a nurse working at Shafa hospital I make a measly wage. Prices go higher and higher every day. To cut things short, I just wanted to beg you to be kind and give us more time so that we will have six more months to repay our debt with interest."

NASSER: *Looks at Nazanine*

"First of all Mrs Afshar, you shouldn't use the word interest. We are committed muslims. God forbid the day that we stoop to usury. This small sum that we charge you is not really interest; it is a fee for our time and trouble that is all. Secondly, do not even mention a delay. You agreed to pay your debt on time. Don't even think about a delay in repayment. You know Haj Fatimeh very well."

He approaches Nazanine

"The money belongs to her. She is counting the days for you to repay her. She is going to cash your cheques on the due date and not a day later. Specially since she doesn't get on with you very well these days."

NAZANINE: *Looking rather desperate.*

"But we don't have enough money in our bank account."

NASSER: *Indifferently*

"No problem. We will refer your cheque to the relevant authorities and we will have your husband arrested if necessary. You must not take advantage of our kindness and friendship. We lent you money and you gave us these cheques. Now, if you repay us on time, then fine, if not, whatever transpires is of your own doing. There is no other way. You know Fatimeh's father very well. I am thinking about Haj Agha Rostami, the powerful Shariah judge of Bardsir. I haven't got a single doubt in my mind that Fatimeh will take your case directly to him should your cheque bounce."

Nazanine seems worried and depressed.

"Where the interests of his daughters are concerned, Haj Agha Rostami could be very unforgiving. He wouldn't know friend or foe. He will turn your life into a living hell. I know him very well. I suggest that you get the money ready as soon as possible so that god forbid your cheque would not bounce."

Nazanine takes a tissue out of her handbag wipes her tears and sobs silently. Nasser looks at her with lust in his eyes and seems content to have succeeded in scaring her desperately.

"You might not be aware of this, but I am sure that your husband Mr. Yazdani very well knows that bouncing cheques is no different from swindling people. God help the poor man. Early in the morning the police will kick your door in and drag your husband outside while kicking and screaming and throw him into Evin prison. He would be their guest for ten to twelve years and believe me dear lady, Evin is no hotel."

Nazanine is sobbing loudly, Nasser looks around, no one has noticed them

NAZANINE: *Turns to Nasser while desperately crying*

"Mr Lotfi, I beg you, please have mercy upon us. Give me a few more

months; we will repay our debt in full. I promise you."

NASSER: *Stays silent*

"Could you possibly help us?"

NASSER: *"Maybe I can persuade my wife to give you another six months. But of course you are also aware that I have known my partner Mr. Sedagat since elementary school. He has a lot of respect for me. Furthermore, Ms Fereshteh is Fatimeh's cousin. I can easily convince my partner Mr Sedagat. He might also agree to give you an extra six months. How does that sound Ms. Nazanine!?"*

NAZANINE: *"May the dear lord give you a long and prosperous life Mr. Lotfi."*

NASSER: *"Ms. Nazanine, I don't want a long life or prosperity. I would be happy with the one I have only with a little more fun and enjoyment thrown in."*

Looks at Nazanine and then goes silent for a short while.

"Maybe you can also do something for me?"

NAZANINE: *Hasn't got the point yet* "Mr Lotfi please believe me I shall do whatever I can. Just promise me not to send my poor husband to jail."

NASSER: *Looks around. The café is not crowded. No one is paying attention to them. He holds Nazanine's hand and begins to rub. He has a wicked grin on his face.*

NAZANINE: *Suddenly realises the situation and quickly withdraws her hand*

"What do you expect from me?"

NASSER: *Looks at Nazanine with a smile.*

"For saving your husband's life, all I require is a couple of hours of your time. Just to spend a little time with each other. Just me and you. Just us."

NAZANINE: *Quickly grabs her handbag off the table and stands.*

"Aren't you ashamed of yourself? I happen to be the wife of a friend of yours for god's sake."

"To hell with this money. Shame on you."

NASSER: *With a smile*

"The choice is yours, ten to fifteen years with hard labour for Mr. Sassan Yazdani, or a couple of hours with me?! You go and think it over carefully and I will call you at 11.00 am tomorrow. Then you can let me know where I stand."

THE WAITING ROOM AT THE COURTHOUSE

Nazanine is sitting next to Sassan. Silence prevails. Arash seemingly continues to read his newspaper. A few people are pacing around the hallway.

SASSAN: *"Speak in an elaborate and refined tone."*

NAZANINE: *Clears her throat.*

"My father Colonel Afshar was very well respected during the Shah's rule. We lived very well. We had servants to do our chores. My father was only steps away from becoming a general. Also, my uncle Mr Sadeq Afshar owned many confectionary stores across Tehran. He was financially very well off. He owned two houses in Tehran and a nice villa in Ramsar along the Caspian coast. My cousins Hadi and Soheil were both top students at Tehran University. But they were both arrested and accused of politically subversive activities against the Islamic Republic regime and jailed as anti-revolutionaries. My poor uncle spent millions and paid off many officials to prevent his sons from being executed. He sold everything he owned. But to no use. In the end, not only did they execute my cousins, but they arrested and jailed my uncle for a couple of months."

"Your honour, when my uncle was finally freed from jail, he was determined to get his younger son and daughter out of the country whatever it took, and to send them to the United States to continue their education. Since he didn't have much money left, he gave cheques to people and borrowed enough money to send Mohsen and Sepideh to America despite all the trouble he went through. We paid a heavy price for the bad cheques that he had written. He was hiding for a while. They were looking for him everywhere. His picture was printed in the newspapers as a wanted fugitive from the law and his arrest warrant was issued. One early morning, before I went to school I was having breakfast in the kitchen …

COLONEL AFSHAR'S HOUSE – TEHRAN

ONE YEAR AFTER THE REVOLUTION – 7.30 AM

Maliheh, Colonel Afshar's wife sets breakfast that consists of a few pieces of traditional Iranian bread, some cheese and a pot of tea on the table. She is in her early thirties. Their daughter Nazanine who is now six years old is sitting at the table and waiting for her breakfast. The phone starts to ring. Colonel Afshar, 45, leaves the bathroom wearing white pyjamas. He is cleanly shaven. He walks toward a small table where the phone is and picks up the receiver.

COLONEL AFSHAR: "*Yes, hello, who is this? Is that you Sadeq? Where are you? Yes, yes I will be home come on over I will see you here.*"

The Colonel seems shocked and very worried.

MALIHEH: *Leaves the kitchen holding a plate full of vegetables and walnuts.*

"*Who was it this early in the morning?*"

COLONEL AFSHAR: "*It was Sadeq, my brother.*"

MALIHEH: "*You know that they are after him and looking for him everywhere. What did he want?*"

COLONEL AFSHAR: *He needs money. He wants to flee the country as soon as possible.*

MALIHEH: *Anxious and worried.*

"*Don't get involved Colonel. This is dangerous. You were sacked from your job, you don't have an income anymore.*

COLONEL AFSHAR: *Tries to persuade his wife.*

"You very well know that Sadeq has never asked me for anything all of his life. Quite the opposite, he has always helped us out when we needed it. Every summer he would let us use his villa on the Caspian. My dear, we mustn't let him down in this desperate situation. Furthermore, should he be able to reach America and get with his children he could become a refuge for us in the future. Listen my dear, Sadeq is a shrewd man. Should he get to America, I am sure he will start anew, maybe a business, he will be successful and able to give us a hand in the future should we ever need it. Maybe we can all go to the U.S someday. What hope do we have left living in this dump of a Islamic Republic? Just look at our young daughter, what kind of a future can she look forward to under the Mullahs."

MALIHEH: *Stays silent, she seems convinced.*

"Where is Sadeq now?"

COLONEL AFSHAR: *Looks at his watch.*

"He should be here in a few minutes. You had better go fetch two hundred thousand tomans from the basement safe. I will go and leave the front door open so that he wouldn't have to ring the bell. I don't want the neighbours to know that he is here."

Maliheh goes to the basement and the Colonel walks towards the front door, opens it and returns inside. Maliheh returns with a bag full of money. The sound of the front door being shut is heard. Sadeq enters the room looking unkempt, wearing a long beard his hair all dishevelled.

SADEQ: *"Good morning. "*

Walks towards the Colonel while sobbing and kisses his hand.

COLONEL: *Tries to console him.* *"The money is ready."*

He points to the bag on the table.

MALIHEH: *"Come and have a quick breakfast before you leave."*

SADEQ: *"Thank you, but I had better leave as soon as possible."*

He takes the bag of money. Suddenly the doorbell rings.

COLONEL: *"This must be the postman (Turns to Sadeq) but just to be safe you better wait in the basement."*

Sadeq puts the money back on the table and dashes towards the basement. Maliheh waits in the living room as the Colonel goes to answer the door. As he opens the door a bunch of revolutionary plain clothes militia storm inside and drag the Colonel into the living room. Nazanine screams as she witnesses this scene. The Colonels wife is terrified. They cuff the Colonels hands behind his back.

MALIHEH: *Walks towards the armed intruders.*

" Please let him go."

Hashem the gangs leader punches her face and she collapses onto the floor. The militants continue to violently beat the Colonel. The Colonel has blood all over his head and face. They verbally abuse him.

HASHEM: *"You anti-revolutionary bastard. Traitor. We are going to mess you up. Where is he? Start to talk. Where is he?"*

SADEQ: *He comes out of the basement, everyone falls silent at his sight.*

"It is me you are after! Here, I am yours; for god's sake let these people go. They are all innocent."

Hashem goes to Sadeq and slaps him so hard that he falls on the floor. At his gesture one of his men hand cuffs Sadeq. Meanwhile, the bag of money captures Hashem's attention. He picks up the bag and looks inside. He walks towards the Colonel who is kneeling on the floor.

"You anti-revolutionary traitor. You old regime cronie. You were planning to give this money to those who are plotting against the revolution weren't you."

COLONEL AFSHAR: *In a desperate tone.*

"Please let me explain."

HASHEM: *With a smile.*

"Your explanation isn't at all necessary. We have been listening to your phone conversations for quite a while now."

SADEQ: *In a whimpering and shaky voice.*

"This money is for me. I wanted to borrow it from my brother to pay my debts. I wanted to pay people back and collect the cheques I have left with them. There is no more to it than that. Please believe me. You must know how much money I owe people."

HASHEM: *Walks towards Sadeq who is kneeling on the floor and kicks him in the face. Sadeq falls on his back.*

"Shut up. We are going to hang you like we did your anti-revolutionary sons. You take people's money to help the anti-revolutionists and instead (as he shouts) you write bad cheques. You sold your country you are a bloody traitor."

He walks toward the Colonel.

"You must give us the names of all your collaborators'."

He gestures with his hand.

"Take these traitors away."

The militants drag Sadeq and the Colonel out of the house. Maliheh, the Colonel's wife has passed out on the floor. Nazanine is sitting in a corner in shock. She is tightly holding a rag doll and singing it a lullaby.

NAZANINE: *"Hush my little baby, don't you cry, hush little baby don't you sigh, soon my little baby good will be by, hush my little baby don't you cry?"*

NAZANINE AND SASSANS HOUSE

MIDNIGHT – IN THE BEDROOM

Nazanine is wearing a long night gown and lying in bed. On the other side of the bed Sassan seems to be in a deep sleep with his back to Nazanine. Nazanine has her hands under her head, is lying on her back staring at the ceiling. She turns toward Sassan whose loud snore can be heard.

NAZANINE: *She mutters.*

"Poor man. He works so hard that he looks like the walking dead when he gets home and collapses on the bed. He worries so much. The concern and responsibility of these cheques is crushing him. He is wilting like a trodden flower. What more can he do? How could anyone work any harder than this?"

She quietly sits up on the bed and lovingly looks at Sassan, his face lit in the pale light. Sassan is deep asleep. She mutters to herself.

"This man has a heart as big as the sea. He is nothing but kindness and affection; he is all I have in this world."

She takes a deep breath.

"I love him more than the whole world put together. I worship him"

She pauses for a moment.

"My dear lord is my witness, since the day we got married; I haven't kept a single thing from this man. I have confided everything with him."

She pauses for a moment

This bastard Nasser Lotfi, this low life, weasel, disgusting example of a man who claimed to be Sassans friend, look how he tried to take advantage of our desperation. Well the bastard has badly miscalculated. He doesn't know me yet. First thing tomorrow morning, before Sassan leaves for work, I am going to tell him exactly what happened. He is very protective; he will give him what he has coming to him. He will teach him a lesson that will be told in legends. He will make such an example of him so that no other man will ever again even think of going after other people's wives.

Nazanine closes her eyes and begins to imagine.

NAZANINE AND SASSANS HOUSE

IN THE KITCHEN – 7.30 A.M

NAZANINE: *There is a small table in the kitchen with two wooden chairs on either side. Sassan is sitting opposite Nazanine and finishing his tea. Nazanine holds Sassans hand and looks into his eyes.*

"My love, do you have a few minutes, there is something I wanted to tell you."

SASSAN: *A little surprised.*

"Why! Has something happened?"

Nazanine stays silent.

"What's going on, speak?"

NAZANINE: **"**I saw Nasser Lotfi yesterday. I wanted to discuss our debt with him."

She looks down as if in shame and continues after a long pause.

"I asked him if it was possible for him and his partner Shahin Sedagat to give us another six months."

She gets off the chair, turns away from Sassan and starts to cry. Sassan stands up and puts his hand on her shoulder.

"You would never believe the indecent proposal that this nasty horrible man made to me. He asked me to sleep with him. He has a wife and two children. He must be ashamed of himself."

SASSAN: *He explodes with anger and screams.*

"I am going to kill the bastard."

He storms out of the house and Nazanine quickly grabs her head scarf and runs after him.

SHAHID DADBIN STREET

OUTSIDE LOTFI & ASSOCIATES EXCHANGE BUREAU

SASSAN: *Sassan storms into the Bureau. Nazanine approaches the place. Sassan is punching Lotfi in the face as he is holding him by the neck.*

"I will kill you, you back stabbing mother...., you piece of shit, you bastard. How dare you go after my wife?

Passers-by gather around them, Nasser smashes Lotfi's head against the trunk of a tree outside the shop. Nasser is bloodied all over. Sassan finally lets him go. Nasser collapses on the pavement. The crowd starts to scream murderer, murderer, don't let him get away. Fatimeh, Nasser's wife arrives on the scene. She starts to scream as she tries to reach her husband. She holds him in her arms as she kneels next to him and turns and looks at Sassan and Nazanine.

FATIMEH: *Cries angrily as she holds up her bloody hand for all to see.*

"I demand retribution. I want vengeance. An eye for an eye a tooth for a tooth!"

In the meantime Shahin Sedagat and Haj Agha Rostami and his two guards break into the circle of the crowd. Nasser Lotfi is lying on the pavement and Fatimeh is holding his head on her lap. Sassan and Nazanine are standing by somewhat bewildered. With a gesture from Haj Agha Rostami, the revolutionary guards go toward them.

SASSAN & NAZANINE'S HOUSE

IN THE BEDROOM – MIDNIGHT

NAZANINE: *She can't sleep, she takes a few deep breathes and continues to stare at the ceiling. She can still hear Sassan's snores. Nazanine thinks aloud muttering to herself.*

"No. No. It won't be right. It won't be for the best. I must never let Sassan find out about this." *Panics* "I just won't pick-up the phone when Nasser Lotfi calls tomorrow. Let him think that I am not home. It is better this way." *She seems unsure* "Even that won't be necessary. This dirty animal doesn't scare me. Maybe it is better for me to talk to him and tell him how wrong he is. Tell him to get these evil thoughts out of his head. Remind him that he is married, that his father-in-law happens to be a man of the cloth for god's sake. Tell him to repent, remind him that it is a deadly sin to covet other men's wives. Particularly your friends wives."

A few minutes pass by

"I really don't know what to tell him. Will these words even get through to someone like him? Someone who obviously has no scruples, let alone a conscience. Maybe he would be offended and angry. Then he will put the cheques into the bank and advise his partner Shahin to do the same and get us in real trouble. When the cheques bounce they will take legal action and then they will get an arrest warrant and break into our home early in the morning like he said.

She looks at Sassan again and delves into her thoughts.

SASSAN AND NAZANINE'S HOUSE

VERY EARLY IN THE MORNING

The doorbell won't stop ringing. Nazanine leaves breakfast on the small table in the kitchen and goes toward the front door to open it. Shouts and screams can be heard. Sassan, who is wearing a set of white pyjamas leaves the bathroom. Hashem the leader of the local militia and his gang whom Nazanine very well remembers from childhood break into the house and attack Sassan punching and kicking him violently. Nasser Lotfi and Shahin Sedagat follow them into the house. Nazanine tries to defend her husband by placing herself between the militia and Sassan.

NAZANINE*: While shouting and screaming "You murderer, let him go. You are killing him. What the hell do you want from us?" Hashem violently slaps Nazanine on the face. Nazanine's nose starts to bleed. She falls onto the floor. Nasser and Shahin look on. The militia tie Sassan's hands behind his back.*

HASHEM*: Takes two cheques out of his jacket pocket and faces Sassan who is being held on his knees*

"You thief, you cunning man. You think you are very clever, don't you? You borrowed money from these gentlemen under false pretences and gave them these bad cheques. Who do you think you are? We are going to mess you up. We will throw you into Evin Prison. You can rest assured, you will never leave that place alive. You will rot in there and then go straight to hell."

Turns to his cronies

"Take this thief and swindler away."

NAZANINE: *Begging and sobbing.*

"Please don't do this. My husband is not a thief. He is not a swindler.

Hashem, the militia, Sassan and Shahin all leave the house. Nazanine is lying on the floor. Nasser approaches her and stands over her. Nazanine looks up. Nasser looks at her with a victorious grin on his face and leaves.

NAZANINE: *"Hush my little baby, don't you cry. Hush little baby don't you sigh, soon little baby good will be by, hush my little baby don't you cry."*

NAZININE AND SASSAN'S HOUSE

MID-NIGHT - BEDROOM

Nazanine quietly gets out of bed and walks to Sassan's side, she stares at him for a while and begins to stroke his hair. She begins to think.

NAZANINE: *"Dear god why doesn't this nightmare end. Why doesn't this long night turn to day."*

A thought runs through her head, but it is as if she is too scared to even ponder it. She gets up and slowly walks towards the kitchen and quietly closes the bedroom door behind her.

NAZANINE AND SASSAN'S HOUSE

THE KITCHEN - MIDNIGHT

She pours herself a glass of water and sits at the kitchen table. She takes a sip of water. Takes a deep breath and blankly stares at a point in the distance. She begins to mutter again.

"What avenue is left to someone like me? I am so desperate. To save my husband I can do nothing else but to give up my chastity. Naturally Nasser is not going to discuss this with anyone. Then he will be in the same quagmire as I. Then we will sink and drown together."

"I will just pretend to be dead for the short while that he comes over. I will go numb. I will give up my purity and chastity for my husband. There is no other way."

NAZANINE AND SASSAN'S HOUSE

BEDROOM – MIDNIGHT

Nazanine enters the bedroom and sits on the floor facing Sassan and begins to weep quietly.

SASSAN*: "What is it my love? Why are you crying?"*

He climbs off the bed

"What's happened?"

NAZANINE*: "I had a bad dream. A terrible nightmare."*

NASSER LOTFI AND FATIMEH'S HOUSE

SUNDAY – 11:00AM

Nasser Lotfi's house is quite modern. Fine hand woven Persian carpets adorn the floor of every room. A large television set is placed at the corner of the living room. A few fine paintings hang on the walls. Nasser Lotfi is dressed. He looks at his watch. It is a few minutes before eleven. He switches the TV channels aimlessly. He seems impatient and worried. He stops on a movie channel and places the remote on the side table. He takes a pack of cigarettes out of his pocket. He flicks his lighter a few times and tries to light it, but is unsuccessful. His lighter is out of gas. He walks by the large dining table and walks into a large kitchen. He lights his cigarette on the cooker's gas flame. Pours himself a glass of water from the fridge and takes a sip. He places the glass on the kitchen table and returns to the living room. He picks up the phone and sits on the couch. He takes a drag from his cigarette. He looks at his watch again. It is exactly 11:00am. The TV is loud.

Just then Fatimeh enters the kitchen from the door that opens into the garden. The television can be heard. Fatimeh is wearing a black head scarf and a brown light weight coat. She opens the fridge door and places some meat and fruit inside. In the meantime the television suddenly falls silent, Nasser Lotfi's voice grabs Fatimeh's attention.

NASSER: *Lying on the couch and holding a wireless handset in his hand.*

"Hello lovely Miss Nazanine – how are you? I hope I haven't called at a bad time."

Nasser is speaking loudly, Fatimeh has become very curious. She closes the refrigerator door and quietly enters the dining room. The living-room door is open. Fatimeh sees Nasser, but Nasser has his back to the dining-room and can't see Fatimeh. Fatimeh starts to listen.

"Believe me since ten this morning I have looked at my watch a hundred times to make sure that I will call you right on time. Lovely Miss Nazanine please listen to me, as I promised you before, this will stay between me and you. You can also rest assured that Ms. Fatimeh will not object once I decide on something. Understood? So we have an understanding. I will fix everything. But remember sweetie, you must take care of me too. I swear on Haj Fatimeh's life who means the world to me."

Fatimeh is standing only a few feet away listening, Nasser cannot see her with his back to her lying on the couch.

"You and Sassan are going to cost me and my partners a lot of money. Do you realize what it costs to postpone the cashing of these cheques for six months? Money doesn't grow on trees you know. I swear we worked hard for this money." *He laughs*

"These few hugs and kisses are going to cost me an arm and a leg, money that poor Fatimeh has saved little by little at a time." *He laughs.* "But my dear for you anything is worth it."

Fatimeh is in shock. She takes a few steps back towards the kitchen. She accidentally knocks over a glass that is on the kitchen table and breaks it. She quickly hides herself inside a large walk-in closet nearby.

NASSER: *"Hold on for a second."*

Nasser enters the kitchen and sees the broken glass. He looks into the yard through an open kitchen window. He notices an alley cat walking around the garden. He closes the window shut.

"Sorry Ms. Nazanine, someone had left the kitchen window open and a cat got in and broke a glass....who cares, I would break a thousand glasses for one kiss from your lovely lips. O.K. I have to go. I will see you in your house at 3:30 this afternoon. Take care, bye."

Nasser hangs up the phone and leaves the kitchen. After a minute the sound of the front door to the house closing is heard. Fatimeh opens the closet door and comes out into the kitchen distraught and upset. A carving knife and a wooden board lie on the table. Fatimeh picks up the knife and hits the board so hard that the tip of the knife breaks cutting her hand badly. Blood gushes out of her hand. She screams with anger and pain. She wraps a kitchen cloth around her hand and immediately goes into the living room. She picks up the phone and dials a number.

FATIMEH: "Hello, Fereshteh? Are you alone? Could you talk?" *She is sobbing.* "No – I am not at all well.....I couldn't explain on the phone.... Nazanine and Sassan are destroying both of our lives." *She continues to cry.*

"Fereshteh, I must see you as soon as possible....let me tell you this much for now, we must watch Nasser and Shahin around the clock from now on. We must follow them wherever they go. Come over quickly and I will tell you what is going on. I am waiting for you, come quickly."

Fatimeh hangs up the phone. She impatiently paces around the room. She picks up the phone again and dials another number.

FATIMEH: "Hello....I would like to speak with Haj Agha Rostami....what do you mean he is busy? I am his daughter Fatimeh. No, no way"

She is sobbing.

"I must talk to father right this minute....fine I will hold..."

A short pause.

"Father, you've got to help me father....you must return to Tehran right away....no dad" *She is weeping loudly.* "next week is much too late. No dad, I couldn't tell you over the phone. It is too personal....no, no, no.... don't mention anything to Nasser at all....I must speak to you face to face first....the day after tomorrow? You couldn't come sooner? O.K. very well then. I guess I have no choice but to wait until then. I will see you soon dad. Thank you dad."

The doorbell rings. Fatimeh goes toward the front door and opens it. Fereshteh wearing a brown scarf and dark coat enters the house. Fatimeh embraces her while sobbing and whimpering.

LOTFI AND ASSOCIATES EXCHANGE BUREAU

TUESDAY – 10:00AM

Nasser Lotfi and Shahin Sedagat – a 45 year old man wearing a dark suit and a white shirt with dark tidy hair are sitting at their desks in a small office. A 25 year old young man wearing a suit opens the door to the office and enters carrying a tray. He takes the cups of tea off the tray and serves them.

HOSSEIN: *"This is Ahmad tea. Freshly brewed."*

SHAHIN: *"Thank you Hossein. There is some private business Mr Lotfi and I need to discuss, make sure nobody will enter the office unannounced. If you could, deal with the customers yourself and if not have them come back in a few minutes."*

HOSSEIN: *Yes sir Mr. Sedagat, don't worry, you take care of your business, rest assured until you do, no-one will enter this office."*

Hossein leaves the office.

SHAHIN: *Turns to Nasser while stirring his tea.*

"Well well my dear old friend I understand that you have been busy?! You took care of Ms. Nazanine and had a pretty good time?! I thought we were partners? Aye? Friends since school?

"Didn't we share everything since we were kids? Didn't we go everywhere together? Didn't we establish this Exchange Bureau together? Didn't we lend the money to Yazdani together? Now all of a sudden you forget me and go it alone? While smiling. Well my friend alright go have your fun, but this ain't the way to go!"

NASSER: *Smiling "Come on, give me a break. What do you expect? For me to take you along?*

Jokingly

I wasn't going to the movies you know?

I had to work on this for a long time, it wasn't easy you know. At 11:00am when I called her she still would not relent. It took a lot of effort and cunning my dear old friend. Some of us have it and some of us don't. You have to learn to live with it."

They both start to laugh out loud.

SHAHIN: *"Well thanks a lot my old friend. I thought you knew me better than this. Are you then saying that I am slow or something? Not as good as you, is that what you're saying?"*

Nasser shakes his head in disagreement.

Nasser falls silent for a short while. He is thinking to himself and shaking his head. He lights a cigarette and after a few seconds

SHAHIN: *"Nasser, would you like to make a bet?"*

NASSER: *Surprised "Make a bet with you? On what?"*

SHAHIN: *Takes a sip of tea. "I bet you that I can have Nazanine after one single phone conversation."*

NASSER: *"Not in your life. Keep on dreaming my friend. There is no way she will have you. In any case there is no reason for her to. I promised her that I will persuade you to go along with the deal. Don't go and belittle yourself with her for no reason. She is not going to do it."*

SHAHIN: *I will give her a good enough reason. You leave it up to me. Just tell me are you in on the bet or not?"*

NASSER: *O.K. but if you lose don't you expect to get your money back." Pauses. "O.K. what's the bet?"*

SHAHIN: *"Two hundred thousand tomans. I will call her right in front of*

your eyes and setup a date with her for tomorrow. You can listen on the other phone. Just don't say anything. One word from you and you lose the bet. How about it? Are you in?"

NASSER: *"No, not two hundred, let's double it. Let's make it worthwhile. Four hundred thousand or nothing at all."*

SHAHIN: *"Very well then"*

He extends his hand towards Nasser.

"Let's shake on it. You are on."

NASSER: *"I won't shake on it until I see some money on the table."*

He reaches into his pocket and throws four hundred thousand on the table.

SHAHIN: *Reaches into his coat pocket and takes out two hundred thousand in cash.*

"Here is two hundred in cash and here is another two hundred in traveller's cheque's. Four hundred all together."

NASSER: *"I am not messing with you. If you lose don't come begging for your money back. Forget about it before it's too late."*

SHAHIN: *"Don't you worry my friend. Even if I lose what's a measly 400 thou between friends. It won't be going far."*

He says jokingly

"Anyway who says I am the one that will lose the bet? If I lose it's only money. If I win I will have won the key to heaven's door!"

Nasser takes the money off the table and places it in a paper envelope and seals the bag. They both sign the envelope.

SHAHIN: *"Please put the bag in the safe."*

They light heartedly shake each others hands. Nasser places the money in the safe and then locks it.

SHAHIN: *Picks up the phone*

"What's her number?"

Nasser while smiling takes a number that is written on a piece of paper out of his pocket and hands it to Shahin. Then he goes to his desk and picks up the receiver while excitedly anticipating the upcoming conversation.

Shahin begins to dial the number.

SASSAN AND NAZANINE'S HOUSE AND EXCHANGE BUREAU

TUESDAY – 10:30AM

Nazanine is busy dusting and house cleaning. The phone rings. She picks up the phone. She recognises Shahin Sedaqet's voice.

SHAHIN: *"Good morning Ms. Afshar I hope you are well....yes it is Shahin Sedagat.....I just heard from Nasser that poor Sassan suffers from stomach ulcers. I was very upset to hear that. Nasser spoke with me regarding your situation and managed to persuade me to give you six more months so that you will have enough time to save the money you need to pay off your debts. After all we do not want to see your cheques bouncing all over the place do we? God forbid we certainly do not wish to see the police get involved."*

NAZANINE: *"Thank you Mr Sedagat. I am very grateful."*

SHAHIN: *"Of course, in return for the help I am giving you I also expect a small favour."*

NAZANINE: *Quite surprised. "Please go ahead."*

SHAHIN: *"Let me be frank Ms. Nazanine,"*

"I will only be able to help you under the same conditions as Mr Lotfi. I hope that is alright with you."

NAZANINE: *"Under what conditions? Under what arrangements? Long pause. "He must have lied to you. No, no way.....it's impossible."*

Nazanine begins to stutter she is terrified. She sits down. Nasser tries to gesture to Shahin not to talk about the arrangement. Shahin tells him to stay quiet.

LOTFI AND ASSOCIATES EXCHANGE BUREAU

Nasser and Shahin are sitting behind their desks and are each holding a telephone handset in their hands. Shahin is speaking with Nazanine. Nasser is trying to tell Shahin not to refer to his arrangement with Nazanine with a hand gesture. But Shahin puts his finger on his nose gesturing to him to stay quiet.

SHAHIN: *"My dear Ms. Nazanine, Mr Lotfi told me everything quote chapter and verse. I am fully aware of everything that transpired."*

Nazanine is unable to say a word. She continues to sit on the chair. She is holding the phone in one hand and her forehead in another.

"Ms. Nazanine it is not fair for you to discriminate between me and Nasser in this manner. To treat him so kindly and on the other hand to treat me so badly and break my heart. Then to ask me not to cash your cheque and forget about what your husband has done and not to go ahead and report him to the police." He pauses. Well this is totally unfair isn't it? This is a kind of prejudice. The dear Lord will not look at this kindly. Is there any difference between the money I lent you and that which Nasser lent you? Does his money buy more? Or mine less? Answer me Ms. Nazanine."

He tries to convince her, he is talking as if he is the victim who has been taken advantage of.

NAZANINE: *Angry and sobbing at the same time.*

"Mr Sedagat, what now do you want from me?"

SHAHIN: *"Ms Nazanine, I really am not asking for much. All I want is for you to grant me the same favour you granted Nasser. That's all. I know that to save Sassan, you are willing to see Nasser privately for a little while.*

All I am asking for is a little private liaison with you. What is wrong with that my dear? This is a sacrifice you will be making for Sassan, it won't hurt anything. It will remain between me and you. To save Sassan from going to prison you probably should sacrifice a little more. You cannot leave the business half done and hanging in the air."

Nazanine is dazed and befuddled, she is unable to speak and yet couldn't hang up. She is unable to decide what to do.

SHAHIN*: "I promise you and swear on my honour that once this business is done with, both Mr Lotfi and I will go to Mr Yazdani and tell him that we recently found out that you work 17-18 hours a day and yet are unable to repay your debt. We will tell him that we are both aware of the terribly high cost of living and that he is not to be blamed and he can repay us in six months." He falls silent. Nazanine listens intently. "How about that Ms. Nazanine? Is that agreeable?" Pauses "Please answer me?! In this way Sassan could go about his life without having to worry about a single thing. Aren't I right Ms. Nazanine?"*

NAZANINE*: After a long pause and with utter dislike.*

"O.K. then. When are you going to speak to him?"

SHAHIN*: Sounding very happy*

"On Wednesday around 1:00pm. I will come to your place and we will have a little friendly chat. It will be just between me and you. Then later in the evening, before Sassan gets home we shall meet with him and tell him everything that I just told you. You can be sure that he will be very happy. This news would soothe his ulcers faster than any medicine. Don't you agree?"

NAZANINE*: Seems a bit calmer*

"Yes, I suppose you are right. Poor Sassan has been in torment in the past few weeks....O.K. that is fine."

LOTFI AND ASSOCIATES EXCHANGE BUREAU

TUESDAY – 10:30AM

SHAHIN: *Happily hangs up the phone*

"Didn't I tell you" He is laughing out loud

"Nasser my dear man you seem to have underestimated me, after 40 years of friendship apparently you still don't know me very well?!"

NASSER: *"I must confess. You are right. A big bravo. You can hoodwink the devil himself."*

SHAHIN: *"My dear Nasser let's forget the chit-chat and get to the point at hand. You lost the bet old boy. Tally up. Let's have the envelope. I will tell you about the other aspect of the bet later."*

NASSER: *"Well you haven't done it yet. Once it is done, then you can have the money. You never know, she might still change her mind."*

SHAHIN: *"Dear friend. Don't make excuses, as far as I'm concerned. I won and no way she'll change her mind. If it's necessary I'll get her letter of consent and bring it to you."*

LOTFI AND ASSOCIATES EXCHANGE BUREAU

WEDNESDAY 8:00AM

Nasser and Shahin are sitting behind their desks. Nasser is adding some figures on the calculator and entering them into his ledger. Shahin wearing a pin-striped brown suit and wearing pointy metal tipped brown shoes is counting bundles of foreign currency and placing rubber bands around them. Hossein knocks and enters the office.

HOSSEIN: *"Sorry to disturb you, Mr. Yazdani wants to have a few minutes with you in private."*

Nasser and Shahin seem agitated and nervous once they hear Sassan's name. They both become hysterical and speechless. Hossein is surprised to see them act this way.

SHAHIN: *Walks towards Hossein and closes the half open door to the office.*

"Where is he now?"

HOSSEIN: *"He is sitting on that chair – over there! He is insisting that he must see you."*

NASSER: *"What did you tell him? Ha?"*

HOSSEIN: *Seems nervous. "Nothing. What was I supposed to tell him? I told him that you are both busy right now and that if there was anything I could do for him?"*

"He was quite nice. All he said was no thank you I need to talk to Mr Lotfi and Sedagat personally. Did I say something I shouldn't have?"

SHAHIN: *"Go tell him that he has to wait, we are very busy. Tell him it would* *be even better if he could stop by another day when we are less busy."*

Hossein leaves the office and shuts the door behind him. Shahin quickly locks the door from the inside.

SHAHIN: *"Do you think Yazdani is onto us? Did anyone see you go to his house?"*

NASSER: *He seems panicked. He looks apprehensively around him, grabs a chair and places it below the window, he climbs onto the chair and begins to open the window.*

"I think maybe we had better get out through the window just to be on the safe side. This guy might create a scene."

SHAHIN: *"Don't worry, we shall take care of him together."*

He opens the filing cabinet and takes out a club

"I will beat the shit out of him with this. We will claim that he was trying to rob us. We will deny anything that he says."

NASSER: *Closes the window. Puts the chair back where it was before. He sits at his desk and picks up the phone.*

"Hello, Hossein? What did you tell Yazdani?"

HOSSEIN: *He is sitting behind the till. Sassan is sitting on a chair facing him and is chatting with one of the customers. He seems calm and relaxed.*

"I told him that you are busy at the moment. He said that he will wait."

NASSER: *"Did he seem angry or upset to you?"*

HOSSEIN: *"No sir, not at all. As we speak he is chatting with one of the customers. I think they are exchanging jokes, listen, you can hear them laughing."*

NASSER: *"Hold on a second" Nasser turns to Shahin who is swinging a club in the air as if ready to attack someone.*

"Listen batman. Looks like we got it wrong. He is chatting with the customers, he doesn't seem upset at all. Maybe we should have Hossein show him in. Let's see what he wants."

SHAHIN: *"Why not. Have him come in. This miserable bastard sure doesn't scare me!"*

NASSER: *"Hossein show Mr Sassan Yazdani into the office."*

He hangs up the phone.

HOSSEIN: *The office door opens and Sassan Yazdani and Hossein enter the office.*

"Please come in, the gentlemen are expecting you."

Hossein leaves the office closing the door behind him

SASSAN: *"Good morning Mr. Lotfi, Mr. Sedagat, sorry to have disturbed you."*

He shakes hands with both Nasser and Shahin.

Shahin and Nasser look nervously at the bag Sassan is holding. Sassan plunges his hand into the black cloth bag containing the money. As he does Shahin dives under the desk and Nasser hides behind his chair.

SASSAN: Whilst laughing

"What's the matter guys are you playing hide and seek with me?"

NASSER: Shouting

"What have you got in the bag?"

SASSAN: *"This is all the money I owe you. What's the problem?"*

He reaches into the bag and takes out a few bundles of brand new notes and places them on Nasser's desk.

Nasser and Shahin emerge from their hiding places a bit sheepishly. "You were playing a game with me weren't you; it reminds me of when

we were kids."

They all start laughing

SASSAN: Points at the money on the desk

"Here you are. This is my debt to you, repaid in full, including interest, right on time."

NASSER: *Looks at the bundle of cash.*

"God forbid Mr. Yazdani, what interest. Please never mention that word here. Someone might overhear and cause us some trouble. We charge a small commission, that is all."

SASSAN: *With a smile*

"I apologise. Including commission."

Everyone laughs.

Nasser indicates to Shahin. Shahin begins to count the cash.

NASSER: "There was no hurry Mr. Sassan, you still had a couple more days."

SASSAN: "I thank you both from the bottom of my heart. Truly you saved me from the dire straights that I was in. You were a great help."

NASSER: "Mr. Yazdani, this is what we do. There is no greater satisfaction than seeing a happy customer. Specially someone like yourself whom we have known since we were children. An old family friend. Believe me, my father-in-law Haj Agha Rostami asks about you everytime I return to Bardsir for a visit. He asked me to promise him that I will take you back with me next time I go to Bardsir."

SASSAN: "First we must let bygones be bygones and reconcile our wives. Without Nazanine I will not enjoy going back to Bardsir."

SHAHIN: "Thank you Sassan"

Turns to Nasser

"It's all here. To the last penny."

He takes Sassan's cheque out of the safe next to him and places half the money inside. He locks the safe.

"My dear Mr. Yazdani here is your cheque. Your debt is hereby cleared."

He places the rest of the cash on Nasser's desk.

"This is your half, I counted it, it is all there."

Nasser places his half of the money in the safe and returns Sassan's cheque.

NASSER: *Facing Sassan.* *"Truly, there was no real hurry"*

"Please come to us again if you need a loan. We are problem solvers. You are well familiar with our terms and conditions."

SASSAN: *Carefully looks at the cheques, tears them up and puts them in his pocket.*

"This will be my gift to Nazanine. Please rest assured, if I ever again need to borrow money at the highest going rate, I will think of you first."

They all laugh.

SHAHIN: *"Now Mr. Yazdani, we didn't expect any snide remarks from you, right around the corner, Sadeqzadeh Exchange charges 10% more commission that we do. You could go and find out for yourself."*

SASSAN: *"What a heartless bastard he must be."* Laughing. *"Well I was just joking, don't let it bother you."* *Turns to Nasser.* *"May I use your toilet?"*

NASSER: *"Of course"*

He opens a door and indicates to Sassan as he follows him.

"The door at the end of the hallway."

SASSAN: *As he leaves the office.* *"Thanks"*

NASSER: *Goes to the safe. He intends to take the envelope that contains the wager money.*

"Well Mr. Shahin Sedagat it looks like you lost the bet dear old friend."

SHAHIN: *Grabs his wrist:* *"Hold your horses pal, not so fast. There is plenty of time left. It is only 8:30am."*

NASSER: *As he replaces the money inside the safe.*

"Gosh, you sure have some nerve old friend. The poor sod just settled in full."

SHAHIN: *"Yes he paid up, but you still have to give me till the end of the day."*

Sassan returns – they go quiet.

SASSAN:*"Thank you for everything."*

Looks at his watch.

"I have to teach a class at 9:00am. I have to administer a test. I have to correct all the papers by this afternoon. I have a long day ahead."

SHAHIN: *"You look very tired Sassan. Looks like you were celebrating the repayment of your debt with your wife Nazanine last night. Partying late?"*

SASSAN: *"What celebration? I had to take a passenger out of town last night. I got home after 4:00am. Nazanine doesn't even know that I have cleared our debt. I will tell her when I get home tonight. She will be delighted."*

SHAHIN: *Seems ecstatic*

"If I were you, I would take her to Behesht restaurant on Ahmadi Street

They have live music tonight, Mr. Mortazavi will sing for you with his velvet voice until mid-night. Then you can tell her."

SASSAN: *"That might not be such a bad idea. It's been over a year since we went out to eat. All we have been able to do is work, work and save."*

NASSER: *Picks up the phone and gives it to Sassan.*

"If I were you I would let her know immediately and make her happy. Come on, call her now, why keep her worried a minute longer than necessary. Then give the phone to Shahin so that he can thank her for having returned our money in time."

SHAHIN: *Steps between Nasser and Sassan.*

"My dear friend, didn't you hear what Sassan just said? Sassan needs to be at school in 15 minutes. He has to administer a test. Furthermore, one must not rush news like this. She must be relaxed and have time to digest such news next to her husband. This is a private matter Nasser. You had better not interfere. He might not even like to speak with his wife with us present."

He takes the phone from Sassan and replaces it.

SASSAN: *Turns to Nasser*

"I am late. I must run. I will tell her tonight when I get back from work."

SHAHIN: *"Cheers, hope to see you again soon."*

SASSAN: *As he leaves. "Goodbye"*

Shabdar Coffee Shop – Nasiabad Street
Opposite Sassan's Apartment

WEDNESDAY – 12:30PM

Fatimeh is wearing a long brown headscarf, a black light weight coat and dark glasses. Fereshteh is similarly dressed. There are two cups of coffee on the table.

FATIMEH: *As she stirs her coffee.*

"Father has promised to get all of our money back and to punish these pimps. You know very well that daddy knows almost everybody in the judiciary department and as for himself he is a very respected and acclaimed jurist."

As she takes a deep breath "may all this pain and sorrow befall Nazanine and Sassan."

FERESHTEH: *"I hope these low lifes won't cause a big embarrassment in front of the neighbours and drag Shahin and Nasser's names into the mud along with themselves."*

FATIMEH: *Shakes her head*

"Absolutely not. You can rest assured. Father is on top of it. He will manage the situation in a manner that no mention of Shahin and Nasser will be made. My dear Fereshteh, he knows darn well how to deal with them, don't you worry. All we need to do is to follow fathers instructions. He will find out all the shit these two have been up to and form a long and thick case file for them. Then he will organise to prosecute them and we will be rid of them forever."

FERESHTEH: *Looks at the clock on the coffee shop wall, it is 12:40pm*

"You see Fatimeh, do you ever remember Shahin having ever not come home for lunch. Last night I asked him what he would like for lunch tomorrow and he said that he has a meeting and couldn't make it for lunch. Something very fishy is going on. This morning he put on his brand new suit and shoes and didn't even say goodbye when he left. He just slammed the door shut and left."

FATIMEH: *Tries to console Fereshteh*

"They seduced our husbands for money. They deceived them like the little devils that they are. I am willing to swear that both dear Shahin and Nasser will give all for us and the children."

She looks at the clock on the wall again. It is exactly 12:45pm

"They always close the Exchange at 12:30pm to go to lunch and do their afternoon prayers. We must be very vigilant. Let's see if they will come here together. Don't take your eyes off the footpath."

She points with her fingers

"You watch that side and I will watch the other. Watch carefully."

They watch the footpath for a while, suddenly Fereshteh indicates with her finger.

"Oh my god look, it's him, it's Shahin, he has come alone."

They both watch Shahin as he approaches the block where Sassan and Nazanine's apartment is located at. It is around two minutes before 1:00pm. He seems to be pacing around to kill some time. He keeps looking at his watch. He enters the building through the main entrance. As she wipes her tears, Fereshteh places her other hand on her abdomen.

FATIMEH: *Takes her mobile phone out of her hand bag and dials a number*

"Hello dad, Shahin just went inside Nazanine's apartment. He seemed alone. Is Yazdani at school? Are you sure? Then let me call this pimp and give him a piece of my mind. I might feel a little better. Dad, Fereshteh and I can't stand this for much longer. Our hearts are on fire.....O.K. father, I promise.....I will do just as you say.....bye."

Then both ladies pay and leave.

SASSAN AND NAZANINE'S APARTMENT

WEDNESDAY – 1:00PM

Shahin Sedagat rapidly climbs the stairs and stops outside Sassan and Nazanine's apartment. He looks around. There is nobody there. The door is open. Shahin enters and closes the door behind him. He takes off his shoes. He hangs his jacket on the clothes rack at the end of the hallway and enters the bedroom. The curtains are drawn shut. Nazanine, wearing a nightgown is lying on the bed. She turns away as Shahin enters. Shahin unbuttons his shirt.

SASSAN AND NAZANINE'S APARTMENT

WEDNESDAY – 6:00PM

Nazanine is preparing dinner. She is nicely dressed. She takes a necklace out of a box and puts it on. She goes to the mirror and fixes her make-up. She puts on some perfume. She sets two plates and two tall white candles on the small kitchen table. She neatly places the cutlery on either side of the plates. She enters the bedroom, removes the sheets off the bed and begins to cut and tear them into pieces using a pair of scissors and her teeth. She replaces them with new sheets. She keeps looking at her watch. She goes to the window again. It is 6:00pm. Wipes clean a picture frame containing a photograph showing her and Sassan by a pond and puts it back on the table. She hears the door to the apartment open and close. She goes into the hallway. Sassan looking very pale and distraught enters the apartment.

He falls onto his knees upon the apartment floor as if he is suffering from great pain. Nazanine sits on the floor opposite Sassan and stares him in the face. Sassan turns away from her.

NAZANINE: *"What's wrong? Speak to me." Nazanine thinks for a while.*

"I know, those bastards tried to cash the cheque. Have the cheques bounced?"

Sassan doesn't seem to be paying much attention to her and tries to avoid eye contact.

"Sassan, if that is the case, please let us escape and leave this place before they come and arrest you. We could go to Esfahan, Mashad, we could escape to the mountain, the desert. Wherever the hell it is, it would be better than falling into their hands."

SASSAN: *Looks at her suddenly and cuts her off.*

"Do you know what the hell you are talking about? You pretend as if you don't know what is going on."

NAZANINE: *Seems confused. "The cheques. Our debt to Nasser and Shahin Sedagat. Have they reported you to the police. Are they after you?"*

Silence

SASSAN: *Reaches into his pocket and throws the torn up cheques at Nazanine.*

"I repaid our debt first thing this morning. Are you going to continue with this sharade? Aren't you ashamed? Don't you have any dignity? If they are to arrest anyone it should be you. You are the one that should be stoned to death."

He snatches Nazanine's necklace off her neck, tears it apart and slaps her on the side of her face.

"What have I got to live for anymore? With what you have done. I would much rather die." While screaming

"What wrong did I do to you? I did everything to make you happy. You were my all." He is sobbing.

"Why did you break my heart? Why did you crush me?"

Nazanine who suddenly realises that all is revealed seems dazed – she goes to the bedroom.

SASSAN AND NAZANINE'S BEDROOM

7:30PM

NAZANINE*: Looking pale, disturbed and bewildered closes the bedroom door behind her and walks to her dressing table and stands in front of a large mirror that shows the upper part of her body. She stares at herself for a few moments, her long hair hanging down her shoulders. She feels innocent, used, cheated. Her thoughts maybe heard spoken by her image in the mirror.*

"I want to cry, but I am unable to, crying does not heal my pain any longer. I want to cry out from the bottom of my heart and soul. My throat has gone dry, I am choking on my sorrows. I want to speak, but no strength is left in me. There is nothing I can say that will justify my despicable behaviour. My tongue is tied."

She pauses slightly

"I shattered my husband's heart to pieces and my own heart that only beats for him along with it. All I wanted was to grab his hand and prevent him from falling into a quagmire. But instead I pushed him deeper into a dark pit full of poisonous and dangerous vipers where he is faced with the deadly fangs of these snakes whichever way he turns. My only wish was for my husband Sassan to be proud of me. But inadvertently, I turned into a filthy and foul smelling blot of shame, a tempest of doom and humiliation that engulfed my innocent and pure husband into it as well. I brought nothing but shame and degradation upon him.

The foul and rancid stink of my shameful and sinful behaviour shall doubtless be heard all over our neighbourhood. We shall be the talk of the town. I unknowingly dragged Sassan into this ungodly mess. Even

Sassan's parents, brother and sister will now be unable to look him in the face. No other doors remain open to such a destitute, poor and helpless failure as I. All avenues are now closed. What can I do to wash away this shame? This humiliation?"

After a slight pause, she takes a deep and desperate breath and then continues.

"I wish my parents had never brought me into this world. I wish I had never been born. I wish they had taken me with them when they departed for the here-after."

She continues with deep emotion

"What good am I, wallowing in sin, nothing but a fountain from which flows a polluted spring that only leads to perdition. I love Sassan with all of my heart and soul. I worship him. Whatever it takes and at whatever cost I must cleanse him and remove this festering and rancid tumour that is born of my shameful behaviour from him. So that at least from here forth my dear Sassan can continue to live with his head held high, I shall sacrifice my unworthy life in this worthy cause. I shall wash off this filth and scum from him."

She looks at the veins in her wrists

"The blood that is flowing in my veins is all that I have left. I shall shed it all at my husband's feet. With the shedding of my blood I shall cleanse and purify us and give him back his honour. I shall tonight baptize my husband in my own blood."

Nazanine leaves the bedroom and goes up on the roof. She goes to the edge and stands there with her hands extended as if she wants to fly. It is almost sunset. A mild breeze is blowing. The street lights begin to come on one after the other. Nazanine walks to the very edge of the air-conditioning box and gets ready to jump. Sassan hurriedly gets to her, grabs her and pulls her onto him. They fall and roll upon the roof. Nazanine struggles to free herself from Sassan's embrace. Sassan lets her go.

SASSAN: Turns to Nazanine

"Then let's jump together. I couldn't live a day without you."

They both break into tears as they hold each other tight.

WAITING ROOM – COURTHOUSE

10:00AM

Sassan and Nazanine are sitting next to one another on a bench. Arash picks up his briefcase stands and begins to leave as he briefly eyes Sassan and Nazanine. Jeff enters the courtroom and walks towards Arash.

JEFF*: "Would you follow me to the waiting room please. I am going to fetch them and bring them to you. Please, as usual, explain all the court rules and regulations to them.*

They both enter the waiting area, which is a small room about three metres wide and four metres long. A large table is located in the centre. There are some chairs placed around it. He leaves Arash in the waiting room and calls Sassan and Nazanine in his very British accent. Immediately after hearing their names called they approach Jeff and introduce themselves and follow him into the waiting room. Arash is sitting at the table. He takes his notebook out of his briefcase and places it in front of him.

JEFF*: Introduces Arash to Sassan and Nazanine.*

"Mr Sassan Yazdani and Ms. Nazanine Afshar. This is Mr Arash Vaziri, your interpreter."

He says the word interpreter in farsi.

"Did I say it right? How is my Farsi? I practice a couple hours a day."

ARASH*: "Yes indeed. Your Farsi is getting to be very good. Don't forget to study the book I gave you. Your Farsi will be even better once you study that book."*

Nazanine and Sassan seem surprised to see Arash – they seem rather embarrassed.

JEFF: *"I will do my best"* Pause *"By the way, apparently the court is going to go into session a bit late today."*

As he leaves the room

"I will see you later."

SASSAN: *Turns to Arash*

"We didn't realise that you were Iranian. We were told that some lady will be interpreting for us today."

ARASH: *Looks at his watch and writes something in his notebook*

"A lady or man, it doesn't make any difference. An interpreter is an interpreter."

There is silence

NAZANINE: *"Sorry Mr. Vaziri, we had no idea that you were our interpreter sitting next to us. We were just trying to practice some of the things that came to our mind. You see, when they began to question us at the Home Office we got all confused. To be honest, we feel that we said some things that we probably shouldn't have said. As a result our request for asylum was rejected and they said we had to 'appeal'"*

ARASH: *Turns to Sassan and Nazanine*

"How long have you been living here?"

Sassan looks at Nazanine

NAZANINE: *"We came to England about ten months ago. We have been out of Iran for about a year."*

ARASH: *Seems curious*

"How did you manage to leave Iran and get here?"

SASSAN: *"Mr. Vaziri, we had to escape from Iran. It is a long story. I do not want to bore you with it."*

ARASH: *"Jeff, who was here a minute ago said that the court won't go into session for quite a while. We have some time. I am interested to know how you got here. Knowing your story could probably help me to convey* *your case more accurately."*

SASSAN: *Looks at Nazanine. She nods her head as if approving what Arash said.*

"Mr Vaziri, I used to be a teacher. Except for Thursday's and Friday's, I taught Persian at an elementary school and after school I used to work as a taxi driver till late at night. About a year ago, I picked up a passenger near Haft Hoz Square in Tehran around midnight."

HAFT HOZ STREET – NARMAK, TEHRAN

MIDNIGHT

Sassan is driving a Samand,a mid-sized car. He pulls over by the pavement. A passenger gets out and pays him through the driver's side window and leaves. Two men walk toward Sassan's taxi and begin to talk to him.

ABDULLAH: *A large man sporting a thick moustache who speaks with a Turkish accent. He is around forty five years old and is accompanied by Saleh who looks around thirty five-ish. Saleh is shorter and slim.*

"My friend, could you give us a ride to Shah Abdol Azim tonight?"

SASSAN: *"No, I am sorry, I am not going that way. Anyway I am done for tonight and have to get home. I am exhausted."*

ABDULLAH: *"I will pay whatever it takes. I will pay double the fair."*

SASSAN: *"No my friend, thank you, but at this time of night I can't go to that neighbourhood."*

"It is too far anyway. My wife is expecting me soon. She won't be very happy if I am late."

ABDULLAH: *Takes a wad of cash out of his pocket and shows it to Sassan.*

"As I said, I will pay whatever it takes. I am happy to pay double the usual fair."

SASSAN: *"Dear gentlemen, my real job is teaching. I have to be in class first thing tomorrow morning. I need to be able to get some sleep. In any case, it takes several hours to drive to that slum. No thanks, I really won't be able to help."*

ABDULLAH*: Tries to hand the wad of cash to Sassan*

"This is 200 thousand. Take it all."

Sassan looks at the cash. He is surprised. He couldn't decide. Abdullah and Saleh get in the car and sit on the back seat.

IN SASSAN'S TAXI CAB

SASSAN: *Picks up his mobile phone – turns to Abdullah and Saleh*

"Then if I may, allow me to let my wife know so that she won't get worried."

He dials the number

"Hello, Nazanine, I will be getting home a few hours later than usual tonight. Don't wait up for me. See you later."

He looks into the rear view mirror as he pulls out

"You know, my wife won't fall asleep until I get home. She is going to lay awake until I return."

ABDULLAH: *May God bless you both. Thank you so much, you are doing us a great favour tonight. My name is Abdullah, I am grateful. I am from Tabriz, but I was born in Istanbul. I am a truck driver. I carry freight between Iran and Europe. Saleh is my right-hand man."*

SASSAN: *"Nice to meet you. My name is Sassan. Pardon me for asking, but what on earth do you want in that run-down neighbourhood at this time of the night."*

ABDULLAH: *"Well, I am supposed to meet someone over there. If you would, you and Saleh wait for me for a while, I won't be long. You can then drop us back where you picked us up."*

SASSAN: *"No problem" He looks in the rear view mirror. "Do you work from Turkey or Iran?"*

ABDULLAH: *"Both. I load stuff in Turkey for Iran and visa versa. Sometimes from Turkey to Belgium, Germany, Holland, even England."*

*"***SASSAN**: *Seems surprised.*

"That is something good for you. So you get to travel half the world. What

kind of products do you carry from Iran?"

ABDULLAH: *Pauses a bit and tries to look at Sassan through the mirror.*

"Mostly I load dates from the city of Bam, in Kerman province, and take them to Turkey. Why do you ask?"

SASSAN: *"Just curious. I had heard that Iranian ceramic tiles are very popular over there, I thought maybe you carry those too. I know some people in the business."*

ABDULLAH: *"No, I'm not in this trade, just mostly pistachios from Kerman. They are very popular in Europe. Specially in Germany, Belgium and France. It's worth it's weight in gold over there. Towards the end of Autumn that is what I mostly carry."*

SASSAN: *"I hear that customs charges a lot of export taxes for these products."*

ABDULLAH: *"Well, my brother, our pockets are full of money and the customs people are in our pockets." They laugh. "Well, they need to make ends meet too, don't they? One has to spread the wealth. We are not scrooges after all." He looks out the window. "Isn't this Atef Street?"*

SASSAN: *"Yes, that's it."*

ABDULLAH: *"I will give you directions from here. I know this neighbourhood like the back of my hand. Turn right at the next light."*

Sassan does as he asks turning left or right as instructed.

"Pull up outside that confectionery shop. I need to take care of something. I won't be long."

Sassan stops in front of the store. Abdullah gets out of the car and starts to walk toward the store. Abdullah knocks on the door a few times. Someone opens the door and they both walk inside.

SASSAN: *Speaks slowly*

"Do you speak Farsi?"

SALEH: *"Yes sir. I am Iranian. A Persian. But I also speak Azari and Turkish very well."*

SASSAN: *"Abdullah speaks Farsi very well."*

SALEH: *"Because his wife is Iranian. He is a very nice and generous fellow."*

SASSAN: *"Most truck drivers I have run into seem to be of the generous type. They all seem like simple folk. Straight forward. Not like city folk these days."*

Abdullah opens the door to the car and gets back in. He is carrying a box of sweets. He takes the top off and offers some to Sassan. Sassan takes a couple out of the box.

SASSAN: *"Thank you, these are good and very delicious."*

He picks up a box of tissues and offers one to Abdullah.

ABDULLAH: *"Enjoy. It isn't much."*

Sassan starts the car.

"Turn right at the end of this street."

They enter a ghetto-like neighbourhood. There is rubbish piled up on either side of the street. The buildings are mostly abandoned and dark. One could hear dogs barking.

ABDULLAH: *"Stop outside that garage. I will be back quickly."*

SASSAN: *"Abdullah! This is a nasty and dangerous neighbourhood. Most folk don't even walk around here in the light of day. Where are you going? Be very careful. This place is infested with thieves, pick-pockets and drug dealers. Only two or three weeks ago, they found a few headless bodies right on this street. Even stopping the car around here is not such a good idea. Even the police don't venture around here. They are afraid of being robbed!"*

ABDULLAH: *Laughing "Don't you worry my friend. Your buddy Abdullah has been to much worse places than this. This is not the first time I have come here."*

Abdullah says something to Saleh in Turkish and leaves the car.

"I will be back soon."

SASSAN: *Looks at his watch.*

"It is half past one. Couldn't he at least wait till tomorrow morning?"

SALEH: *"He is owed some money that he must collect tonight since we are leaving for Turkey early tomorrow."*

SASSAN: *"What money? Are you serious? People around here don't have two pennies to rub together. Who can collect money from this kind of people. Has he forgotten where he is? These people are hungry."*

"Nobody gives money to anyone around here my friend. God help us all. What did Abdullah just say to you?"

SALEH: *"He said that he will be back in 5 minutes. If not to go after him. He said that he will leave the door open behind him. I had better go take a look, it's almost over 10 minutes now."*

SASSAN: *"Where the hell are you going man? Don't leave me all alone in this fucking neighbourhood. Fuck me."*

SALEH: *Points with his finger.*

"Over there next to that metal gate there is an alley. Just wait right here, we will be back soon. Don't you leave and abandon us now!"

Saleh gets out of the car and turns towards the iron gate that opens onto

a garage. Sassan is very anxious, he starts the car thinking to get the hell out of there, but his conscience won't let him. He turns the engine off and puts the window up. He locks all the doors and turns the head lights off. All of a sudden Saleh comes running and bangs on the window. Sassan puts the window down.

SALEH: *"They are beating Abdullah to death. We must do something."*

SASSAN: *Hurriedly opens the car door.*

"How many of them are there?"

SALEH: *While breathing heavily.*

"There are five or six of them, you wouldn't happen to have a gun, knife or some kind of weapon in your car would you? Open the boot, let me see. If we don't hurry, they will kill him."

SASSAN: *"Have you gone mad? Where the fuck am I supposed to get a weapon from? Of course I don't have a weapon."*

Sassan walks behind the car and pops the boot open. Saleh picks up a wheel spanner. Sassan notices a bunch of fire crackers that a passenger had left behind in the back of his boot. He grabs them. They run toward the dark alley next to the garage. They can hear a commotion from the distance. Five or six men are beating Abdullah. Abdullah has grabbed the hand of one of them who is holding a knife and is struggling very hard not to get stabbed. The rest are kicking and punching him violently. Saleh hits one of the men on the head with the wheel spanner. Sassan lights up and throws the fire crackers into the alley. The fire crackers start to burst. Sassan hides behind the garage door and begins to shout at the bottom of his lungs

SASSAN: *"Stop.....stop.....police! Freeze, nobody moves."*

The men attacking Abdullah rapidly disperse. Sassan and Saleh quickly reach Abdullah who is lying on the ground. They lift him up. His head and face all bloodied. They hurriedly go toward the car. Sassan opens the door. Abdullah and Saleh sit in the back seat. Abdullah is panting and breathing very heavily. Sassan immediately gets behind the wheel, starts the car and drives away. He takes a box of tissues from the dashboard and hands them to Saleh.

SASSAN: *"Clean him up. The dear Lord was with us. We were lucky. We could have all been killed. I told you that this is a dangerous area."*

SALEH: *Carefully wipes the blood off Abdullah's face.*

"Mother fucking bastard. Bloody cowards. One of them had a dagger. If we had got there a minute later it was all over. Thank god his injuries are superficial."

ABDULLAH: *He pulls himself together. Takes the tissue from Saleh and begins to wipe his face.*

"I heard the sound of gunfire. Where did the police go? I heard them shouting freeze, don't move. I thought we were all going to be arrested. Where did they go?"

Saleh and Sassan both begin to laugh out loud.

ABDULLAH: *"What's going on?"*

SALEH: *"Our dear friend Sassan acted like a police squad tonight. He saved your life."*

ABDULLAH: *"I heard grenades exploding, gun fire?" Where did they come from?"*

SALEH: *"Sassan you had better explain yourself."*

SASSAN: *"Abdullah these were all fire crackers. They had been gathering dust at the back of my car for months. A passenger left them behind on the back seat. I meant to throw them out, I don't know why but somehow I never got around to it. I guess they were meant to be, so that I could use them to save your life tonight. Otherwise we would have never been able to handle these murderers."*

He takes a bottle of mineral water from the dash and hands it to Abdullah.

ABDULLAH: *"I like you. You are a clever, intelligent kind of guy. I could handle four of them but there were just too many. Mammad the Wolf was trying to stab me in the back, but I managed to grab his wrist."*

SALEH: *"Was that Mammad the Wolf? I didn't recognise him in the dark. We will take care of the bastard. That piece of shit."*

SASSAN: *"Didn't I tell you that only a bunch of hoodlums and thieves, drug dealers and murderers live around this neighbourhood?"*

"They are not the type who return borrowed money. If you lend to these people you might as well forget about it. One should never deal with this type, let alone lend them money."

ABDULLAH: *"I like you and trust you. You seem to be a genuine kind of guy so I am going to confide in you. After all, I owe you my life."*

After a short pause

"On the face of it we carry dates from Bam in Iran and pistachios from Kerman to Europe, but in reality what we carry is a thousand times more valuable. Our real cargo is opium and heroin. Narcotics are smuggled in

from Afghanistan and we load them up and take them across the border. We know all the guards. The customs people too. They all know us very well. We pay good money. Large pay offs and they turn their heads. Sometimes if we find customers who buy large amounts inside the country we get rid of some of it here. Three weeks ago I delivered 50 kilos of heroin and 100 kilos of opium to these assholes. They were supposed to pay up tonight and you know the rest. Our gang is powerful. You can find all kinds of characters working for us. From police and customs people to revolutionary guards even mullahs and clerics, men of the cloth."

They all laugh.

"All they care about is cash. It is pay as you go so to speak. We give and they take. It's a give and take kind of situation. Bribe money

Looks at Saleh, they both laugh.

"This way not only do they not bother us, but they actually watch out for us. Tomorrow morning I will let Colonel Tavakolli know what happened tonight, I guarantee you, in 24 hours, they will either be dead or behind bars. Stupid bastards, they should have known much better than to fuck with us. Mammad the Wolf is their leader, even if he melts into the ground they will find him and fuck him up. There isn't a rat hole he can hide in. I will tell Colonel Tavakolli to stick his batten up his arse."

Sassan quietly listens, but he's shocked at what he is hearing.

SASSAN: *"Where shall I drop you? The same place I picked you up?"*

ABDULLAH: *Indicates to Saleh and he takes a few large bundles of cash out of a samsonite briefcase and hands it over.*

"I would like you to accept this small gift as a token of my appreciation."

He places the cash on the front passenger seat.

"There is a few million, but compared to what you did for me it's really nothing."

SASSAN: *Apprehensively. "Abdullah, on my mothers soul I am not going to accept a penny of this money. Please take your money, please."*

Abdullah takes the money from the front seat.

"I had heard about your generosity from Saleh. Despite the fact that I owe several million and badly need some money, my conscience doesn't allow me to accept this money from you. I am just glad that I was able to help. To save a fellow human's life. You don't owe me anything. Please do not consider yourself obligated to me in any way. I don't expect anything from you."

ABDULLAH: *"Very well then. But it would please me if I could do something for you. Listen my friend, if you or someone you know ever needs to get out of the country in a hurry let me know. This is something I do. My brother Ghafur lives in Istanbul. He can get you the passport to any country you wish including an authentic visa. This is what he does. He charges a great sum, but for you it will be free of charge. It will be on me."*

SASSAN: *Smiles. "I have nothing to do overseas. I have enough trouble getting along and making ends meet here in Iran."*

"Furthermore, should I ever want to leave I can always apply for a passport, like other people."

There is silence, Sassan pulls over to the side.

"Here we are, god be with you."

ABDULLAH: *He hands a piece of paper to Sassan.*

"This is my mobile number. Promise not to throw it away, keep it somewhere safe. You never know, you might need it one day. I mean it, if you ever need anything, if there is ever anything I can do for you

please do not hesitate to call me."

SASSAN: *"Alright. I appreciate it. Although I don't think that day will ever come, nevertheless I will keep it."*

ABDULLAH: *"Put it in the glove compartment of your car right now."*

Sassan places the piece of paper in the glove compartment.

"Maybe we will meet again someday. Take care."

Abdullah and Saleh shake Sassan's hand and say goodbye. Sassan drives away. Moments later he notices a bundle of cash on the back seat. He hits the break. Gets out of the car and looks around. There is no sign of Abdullah or Saleh. He hesitates a short while. There is no-one around. He looks at the bundle of cash. Looks around again. Gets in the car and drives away.

THE WAITING ROOM AT THE COURTHOUSE

Arash is listening to Sassan's story in disbelief. He seems touched by the story. He impatiently awaits to hear the rest. Sassan has fallen silent. Arash begins to ask more questions.

ARASH: *"When did you decide to flee Iran?" Pauses "How did you manage to dodge Haj Agha Rostami and his cronies?"*

SASSAN: *Looks at Nazanine. She seems embarrassed, she looks down.*

"That evening when Haj Agha Rostami caught up with me in the park and had that disturbing conversation there was no doubt left in my mind that both he and his sick daughter were meaning to do Nazanine and I great harm. At night when Nazanine came clean on what had been going on I looked out the window and..."

NAZANINE & SASSAN'S HOUSE

WEDNESDAY – 9:30PM

SASSAN: *Anxiously peaks through the window at a suspicious looking bearded man leaning against a lamp post and staring at the front door to Sassan's apartment block catches his attention.*

"Put the light out right away."

Nazanine quickly switches the light off. The room falls into darkness. Sassan pulls the curtains lightly aside and looks at the bearded man.

"It's him. He works for Haj Agha Rostami. One of his cronies."

He quickly pulls the curtains shut.

"Turn the light back on."

Nazanine switches the light on.

"We must escape and leave this place tonight. Rostami has his people watching us."

Turns to Nazanine.

"We are under surveillance."

NAZANINE: *She is petrified*

"What on earth are we going to do?"

SASSAN: *"If we don't get away tonight Haj Agha Rostami and that bitch of a daughter of his are going to skin us alive."*

He aimlessly paces around the room. He looks through the curtain again. The bearded man is still there.

"Yes, there is no doubt about it. It's him."

Suddenly he remembers Abdullah. He is overjoyed.

"Nazanine I must go fetch a phone number from the glove compartment very quickly. Pull the curtains open, let them think we are at home.

Don't turn the lights out. I will be back very quickly."

NAZANINE: *Anxiously. "Please come back quickly, before I have a heart attack."*

SASSAN: *As he leaves "Don't worry I'll be right back."*

Sassan slowly opens the door and peeks inside the hallway. There is no-one there. He leaves and quietly climbs down the stairs. He goes to the bin store. He opens the door and walks between the wheelie bins, some stray cats, which are scavenging through the bins, quickly jump out of the bins and run under the door which leads out onto the street. He quickly opens the door to the street and heads toward his car which is parked about 100 metres away. He opens the passenger door and takes the paper containing Abdullah's phone number out of the glove compartment. He quickly but quietly closes the car door and goes back to the apartment via the same route. Nazanine seems very happy to see him.

NAZANINE: *"Did you find the number you were looking for?"*

SASSAN: *"Yes I did."*

He begins to dial a number on his mobile phone.

"I hope to god that he answers."

Nazanine sits next to him.

"He picked up.....Hello.....Abdullah good evening.....I am Sassan Yazdani..... the taxi driver, we were together last night.....Oh please don't mention it I didn't do much.....Abdullah I need your help.....You must save me and my wife we are in deep trouble.....I couldn't explain over the phone. We must leave the country immediately. We don't have much money.....around 60,000 tomans. We don't have any passports either.

For god's sake please help us."

".....No tomorrow will be too late.....by then we'll probably be 6 foot under.....

we are both in real danger.....no Abdullah even if we hide in a cave up on a mountain these bastards will find us. O.K. please write down my phone number 09128327465. Thank you so much.....then I will be expecting your call in a few minutes. Talk to you soon."

Turns to Nazanine.

"Quickly pack the bare necessities for a trip. Also put some food in the bag and take all the money you can find in the house."

NAZANINE: *Listening intently*

"O.K. is the brown bag alright?"

SASSAN: *As he walks to the window*

"Yes, just hurry, we must leave this place immediately."

Sassan carefully looks out the window. The bearded man is pacing in front of the front entrance to the apartment block. Nazanine quickly enters the bedroom and throws some clothes into the bag. She then walks to the kitchen. She takes some bread, dates and walnuts out of the fridge, places then inside a zip-lock bag and throws it in the bag. She gets dressed and goes to the living room. Sassan is still carefully watching the guard through the window.

SASSAN: *"I saw this bastard along with another revolutionary guard walking near the bazaar with Haj Agha Rostami."*

Sassan's mobile phone rings. Sassan quickly answers.

"Is that you Abdullah? Thank you very much.....you are very kind. Both me and my wife are very grateful. Please wait a moment"

Faces Nazanine

"Quickly, get me a pen and a piece of paper. Nazanine rushes to get a pen and paper from the table, next to the phone, and hands it to Sassan. Yes, yes, go on Abdullah. I am writing it down."

Sassan quickly jots down a few names and numbers.

"Let me repeat the number one more time, 0912218876. Yes this is a border guard Colonel Amiri's phone number. Did I get it correctly....thank you very much.....let me write your brother Ghafur's phone number down also."

Sassan begins to write again.

"Let me repeat 00905442285945, is that correct? You have my number, very well, I will call you if need be.....yes we will leave tonight and tomorrow evening I will contact Colonel Amiri. Thank you so much for your kindness."

Sassan turns off his mobile phone and places it in his pocket. Turns to Nazanine.

"Are you ready? We must leave immediately. We are going to get out onto the street through the bin store. Just follow me. Leave the light on, let's go."

NAZANINE: *"I am ready, I put 45,000 tomans in my bag, let's go."*

Sassan quickly grabs his bag and carefully opens the door to the apartment, looks down the stairs, there is no-one there. With Sassan's indication Nazanine quietly closes the door to the apartment and follows Sassan down the stairs. As they walk down, they run into one of the neighbours who begins to exchange pleasantries. They try to dodge him unsuccessfully.

Finally they separate and anxiously climb down the stairs and reach the

ground floor. They walk toward the bin store. Sassan opens the door and tries to manage his way around the large wheely bins and onto the street. Nazanine follows. They open the door to the back of the room and enter the almost deserted back street. A few passers-by can be seen. Sassan carefully walks along the pavement and approaches his car. He looks around. Nazanine looks scared, she nervously follows. They reach the car, Sassan looks around then quietly opens the car door. He throws the bag on the back seat. Nazanine sits on the passenger seat next to Sassan. Sassan starts the car and drives away.

BAZARGAN BORDER CROSSING

THURSDAY – INSIDE SASSAN'S CAR

SASSAN: As he drives "So far so good, thank god."

About 200 metres ahead a long line of passenger cars and buses can be seen. A large crowd is bustling about. Several soldiers and border guards pass them by in their jeep. Sassan notices a large sign and points it to Nazanine.

"This is the Bazargan border crossing. The borders between Iran and Turkey. Can you see those tall fences?"

Nazanine nods her head.

"That's the actual border line. You can see the Iranian flag flying on this side and the Turkish flag flying on the other. That is the land of Turkey."

Sassan enters the large parking lot and parks his car. They both get out of the car.

"I must call Colonel Amiri. He is waiting for our call."

NAZANINE: *"Then don't be wasting time, call him right away. I am so nervous my stomach is churning."*

SASSAN: *He takes his mobile phone out of the glove compartment and dials a number.....after a few moments*

"Hello, Colonel Amiri? Hello sir.....I am Sassan Yazdani. Yes, right now we are in a large parking lot at the border standing below a huge Nokia billboard."

He looks around

"Yes that is correct, exactly there."

"I am driving a milky white Samand.....very well we will wait for your

Excellency right here. Thanks a million, see you soon."

Turns to Nazanine

"The Colonel was so respectful and polite. He will be here in one or two minutes. Check everything, make sure we don't leave anything behind. Zip up the bag tight and get it out of the car."

Nazanine takes the bag out of the car, places it on the ground and stands by Sassan's side.

SASSAN: *"Nazanine, look at that long queue. It's unbelievable. It must be three to four kilometres long. One end is at the border. God knows where the other end is."*

NAZANINE: *Looks at the very long queue*

"God help us. I suppose we will have to wait in this queue for several hours before it will be our turn."

Turns to Sassan

"Now I wonder how Colonel Amiri is going to get us through the border with all these soldiers and border guards standing around?"

SASSAN: *Doubtfully "I have no idea. Let's see what he is going to do? Maybe he is going to issue us a couple of passports. What do I know. Just wait, let's see what he suggests."*

In the meantime, Colonel Amiri, a handsome man in civilian clothes pulls over next to them driving a Mercedes and quickly gets out of the car. He greets Sassan and Nazanine warmly and shakes their hands.

AMIRI: *"Hello Mr Yazdani"*

Turns to Nazanine

"Hello Mrs Yazdani. I hope you are not too tired from the trip."

SASSAN: *A bit restive and jittery "Hello sir, this is my wife Nazanine."*

AMIRI: *To Nazanine*

"My dear lady, we have heard of your husband's bravery and gallantry. I had deep respect for him in my heart even before I saw him. I am honoured

and happy to meet both of you."

SASSAN: *Feeling rather humbled*

"Please Colonel. You exaggerate. I am humbled. You are a gentleman. We are both very pleased to have met you."

AMIRI: *Turns to Sassan and Nazanine*

"Abdullah put in a good word for you. Have you had lunch? If not, I am at your service. If you would honour me we can have a chelo kebab together."

SASSAN: *Turns to Nazanine*

"We both had a full lunch, and I am not just saying that."

AMIRI: "Abdullah has carefully scheduled and planned your itinerary. Leave the car right here. Just grab your luggage, give the car keys to my driver and get in the Mercedes."

SASSAN: "All we have is a small bag"

He picks the bag up off the ground. The driver of the Mercedes quickly approaches them. He respectfully takes Sassan's bag and places it inside the boot and opens the car door for Sassan and Nazanine to get in.

AMIRI: *Turns to Sassan and Nazanine*

"Please relax, just get in the back seat and be comfortable. I will personally get you through the border. The driver is one of our own, don't worry about him. You will be fine."

Sassan hands his car keys to the driver and they both sit on the back seat of the Mercedes. Colonel Amiri sits in the passenger seat and they drive away.

INSIDE THE MERCEDES

AMIRI: *Turns round and faces Nazanine and Sassan*

"You are probably aware that we are not allowed to enter Turkey wearing a military uniform. That is why I am wearing civilian clothes today."

SASSAN: *"Yes, I had heard about this before."*

Sassan and Nazanine eye the luxurious and immaculate interior of the Mercedes. Then they look out the tinted windows of the car.

AMIRI: *"We are well acquainted with all the Turkish border guards." Smiles "We help them financially. I mean we make pretty large pay offs and in return, they take good care of us."*

They approach the border. The driver follows a road next to and parallel with the long line of cars and buses waiting to cross. Only border officials are allowed to use this road. Colonel Amiri greets and waves at the officer and border guards along the road as they approach the border area. They salute him as he passes by. The driver slowly passes through the border crossing without even stopping. He gets to the passport control at the Turkish border and enters Turkey. The Turkish officers speak with Colonel Amiri in Turkish. They smile at each other as if they have known one another for a long time. They easily cross the border and enter Turkish soil.

The road is very congested.

AMIRI: *"Mr. Yazdani, how long have you known Abdullah?"*

SASSAN: *With slight hesitation*

"Not for very long, but nevertheless I hold huge respect for him."

AMIRI: *"Abdullah said that he owes you his life! He told us to take the best care possible of you and Mrs Yazdani. He asked us to make* *absolutely certain that you will have the most pleasant trip."*

SASSAN*: "He is very kind. So much kindness has put us to shame."*

He pauses slightly "Are you happy with the work you do?"

AMIRI*: "Of course we are Sassan. The position I hold is in great demand. They don't let just anybody become a chief border guard. We officers pay out one to two million, not million Tomans, one to two million dollars in pay offs alone each month so that they won't take this job away from us. The money is astronomical. You have to be connected and on the inside to be able to do this work. You have to know someone high up. You have to be able and shrewd. A good earner so to speak. After all you are expected to bring in good money."*

SASSAN*: Plays it dumb*

"I have heard that customs charges have gone up"

AMIRI*: Jokingly*

"You don't seem to get it Sassan. What customs charges? Truck loads of antiques, museum pieces, heroin, opium, gold bullion and foreign currency leaves this border every day. Where do you think the tons of heroin used in Europe and the United States comes from? From this very same border crossing. Customs charges? Huh! They pay us to look the other way."

"They let me know the particulars of the truck in question ahead of time. Then we greet them with regard and respect and get them through the border like honoured guests. We pay the Turkish border guard in cash. Last year Mr. Yazdani, they offered to make me a General and position me at the capital Tehran. God is my witness, I had to beg and pay a few people off so that they leave me the heck alone. Thanks to Abdullah and people like him, our income here is higher than any General. We have control over everything that passes through. We take money, millions of dollars and of course pay out millions, at the end of the day we are left with a decent amount."

He turns around and looks at Sassan who is listening with interest.

"I guess you heard about that eighteen wheeler that reached Turkey carrying billions of dollars worth of gold bullion and foreign currency?"

SASSAN: *"Yes, I actually did hear something about that. I heard it on some overseas TV and radio channels. They reported on this in detail. Of course I didn't actually see or hear these reports personally, but many of the passengers in my taxi cab spoke about it. Is this true?"*

AMIRI: *"Yes sir. I myself along with two other officers escorted it across the borders. We were waiting for that eighteen wheeler one week before it reached the border. We were definitely expecting it."*

There is silence. Sassan and Nazanine look at the surrounding landscape through the tinted windows of the Mercedes.

"I think we are here."

He indicates with his finger.

"Pull into that parking lot."

The car enters the parking area.

"Pull along the side of that blue Range Rover."

The driver stops next to the Range Rover. There is a man standing next to the Range Rover. Amiri points to him.

"This is the driver of the Range Rover. His name is Qassem. He is originally from Turkey, but he does understand a bit of Farsi. He will take you to Ghafur, Abdullah's younger brother."

Colonel Amiri takes a stuffed envelope out of his pocket and hands it to Sassan.

"This is from Abdullah, he told me to give this to you. This should cover your trip's expenses. Maybe you would like to purchase some clothes etc. It is around 3000 dollars."

He hands the envelope to Sassan and he reluctantly puts it in his pocket. Amiri, his driver, Sassan and Nazanine all get out of the car. Qassem exchanges greetings with everyone. The driver of the Mercedes takes Sassan's bag out of the boot and hands it to him. Qassem quickly opens the rear door to the Range Rover and politely stands aside.

SASSAN: *Turns to Amiri and takes the envelope containing the money out of his pocket.*

"*Please return this money to Abdullah. He has put us to enough embarrassment as it is. How can we ever return all this kindness.*"

AMIRI: *Pushes back Sassan's hand*

"*No way Sassan. Abdullah will be upset.*"

With a gesture from Nazanine and with some hesitation, Sassan puts the money back in his pocket.

AMIRI: "*When you see Abdullah please remember to tell him that Amiri performed his duties well. I hope that this has been the case?*"

SASSAN: "*Please Amiri, you are underestimating yourself.*"

"*What duty sir. You didn't hold anything back. You showed us every possible kindness in the world. I will definitely let Abdullah know.*"

AMIRI: *Looks at his watch*

"*You must leave before it gets late. Ghafur is patiently waiting for you.*"

Amiri kisses Sassan on the cheeks and says goodbye to Nazanine.

"*If you like and feel more comfortable, you can now take your headscarf off. It's a free country.*"

Nazanine takes off her scarf that has already loosened and fallen around her neck and says goodbye again. Sassan and Nazanine sit on the Range Rover's back seat and close the doors. The Range Rover gets on the way.

GHAFUR'S HOUSE – AN AFFLUENT NEIGHBOURHOOD IN ISTANBUL

Ghafur is a well kept young man in his late thirties. He has black hair, is closely shaven and wearing a neatly pressed shirt and trousers. He is standing on the front steps to a large and beautiful villa and looking toward the iron-gate that opens to the road. A 22 year old servant is sweeping the driveway that leads to the front door from the front gate. Beautifully colourful flower beds adorn both sides of the driveway. Ghafur's mobile phone begins to ring. He takes the phone out of his pocket.

GHAFUR: *"Where are you now?....Very well.....so you will be here in a couple of minutes.....the door is open Qassem.....come right in. I am waiting."*

He opens the front door and shouts

"Golnar, Golnar"

Golnar is Ghafur's young wife. She is thirty years old and nicely made up. She comes out and stands next to Ghafur.

"They will be here in a minute. Abdullah spoke very highly of this couple, we must do whatever we can for them and help them out as needed. We must make sure that they have a good time here. They are going to be our guests for a few days."

"No problem. Nargess tidied up the guestroom, changed the sheets and left them a bowl of fruits on the table. She also cleaned the guest bathroom and left some fresh soap and new towels for them. Lunch will be ready in a couple of hours."

In the meantime the Range Rover pulls in through the large iron-gate

and stops just outside the front door to the house. Qassem rapidly gets out of the car and opens the door for Sassan and Nazanine. Nazanine and Sassan are wearing new clothes. Nazanine is wearing light make-up and is standing next to Sassan. Ghafur steps forward towards Sassan and Nazanine and warmly greets them both and exchanges the usual pleasantries. Golnar shakes hands with both of them. Qassem takes their bag out of the car and Nargess, the maid, takes it inside the house.

GHAFUR: "Mr Yazdani, you and your wife are both welcome in our house. Please come in. I am Abdullah's younger brother. This is Golnar, my wife."

SASSAN: "Please call me Sassan, we are sorry to have troubled you."

GHAFUR: "Please don't say that. What trouble? We were impatiently looking forward to meeting you both. Only if you knew how highly my only dear brother Abdullah spoke of you. I am very happy for the opportunity to meet both you and your wife. Please come in, please."

NAZANINE: Turns to Golnar

"Sorry for the trouble."

GOLNAR: "Not at all, please come in, our home is your home."

They all enter the house and sit in the living room. A few fine and expensive carpets adorn the living room floor. The room is decorated with lavish and stylish furniture. Nazanine and Sassan sit on the sofa. Nargess, a young girl in her early twenties enters the room carrying a tray of cake and tea and serves it to Sassan and Nazanine.

GOLNAR: "Lunch will be ready in a couple of hours. I have prepared Kofteh and Chelo Kebab for you. I hope you like it."

NAZANINE: Thanking Golnar

"Of course we like it. May god bless you both. We are very grateful. You shouldn't have gone to the trouble."

GOLNAR: "Please don't say that Ms. Nazanine. We prepare something for lunch anyway."

GHAFUR: Turns to Sassan

"You seem very tired. You have come a long way. Your room is ready. Why don't you go and rest for a while. Take a shower maybe, freshen up. I will call you when lunch is ready."

THE DININGROOM – GHAFUR'S HOUSE

A variety of Iranian and Turkish meals can be seen on a large dining table. Bottles of coca-cola and mineral water have been placed in front of every guest. Everyone is busy eating and drinking. Turkish music can be heard in the background.

SASSAN: *Stops eating*

"Thank you Golnar, the food was excellent."

GOLNAR: *"You are welcome Sassan."*

Nargess begins to clear the table and carries the dishes into the kitchen. She returns with a nicely decorated plate containing desert and some small plates and places them on the table.

NAZANINE: *Looks at the nicely decorated desert plate*

"You have very nice taste Golnar. This looks wonderful."

Golnar smiles proudly.

GHAFUR: *"Dear Nazanine, compared to what you did for my brother, whatever we do for you fades in comparison. Your husband saved my brother's life."*

"Abdullah told me how your husband's presence of mind saved him from the hands of that knife yielding miserable coward and his gang of murdering hoodlums."

Smile

"Using a bunch of fire crackers at that. Just think about it."

Turns to Sassan who is listening proudly.

"Bravo, what a clever and intelligent mind. Abdullah told me if it was for

a moment later that coward Mammad the Wolf would have stabbed him with his dagger."

SASSAN: *Says proudly* "That was all I could think of under those critical circumstances, the only trick that would work."

He continues excitedly and emotionally

"It was around 1:30am. Saleh and I were impatiently waiting for Abdullah in the car."

Everyone is listening closely

"Saleh told me that he was going to see why Abdullah had taken so long. Saleh got out of the car and disappeared into the dark of the night. It hadn't been but a couple of minutes when he returned looking all frightened and shaken, as you mentioned. He said that a pack of bloody wolves had attacked Abdullah, we had to do something. I immediately got out of the car and popped open the boot. I was looking for a wheel spanner when suddenly I noticed a bunch of fire crackers that one of the passengers had left behind at the back of the car. God knows, they had just been sitting there for at least six months gathering dust. I thought of throwing them away a few times but for some reason never got around to it. It was god's will I suppose. I grabbed the fire crackers, and Saleh picked up the wheel spanner and ran towards where Abdullah was. I followed him and ran after him in the dark."

"We passed through an alley and entered a large yard through the back entrance. Seven or eight pretty large and well built men were beating up Abdullah. Kicking and punching him and attacking him with clubs. Later we found out that a fellow called Mammad the Wolf was their leader. I swear to god Golnar,"

Who is listening intently

"he was carrying a dagger this big."

He shows with his hands

"The blade alone was about half a meter long. Believe me Ghafur despite the darkness you could still see the blade gleam like a night light. Abdullah was holding this murdering bastards wrist as tightly as he could to prevent *him from stabbing him."*

He takes a deep breath.

"Poor Abdullah almost had no strength left in him."

He continues excitedly

"I threw the fire crackers into the alley, they began to go off. They sounded like a machine gun firing. I began to shout 'freeze, stop, don't move, police'. They all suddenly began to scatter like rats. Saleh who hadn't realized what was going on quickly came to me and said 'watch out, duck, the police are firing'."

Everyone laughs

"Then Saleh and I went and got Abdullah who was completely exhausted and lying on the ground and took him to the car."

He pauses for a moment

"Abdullah pulled himself together after a short while and the first thing he asked was where the police had gone?"

Ghafur leaves the dining room and returns with an Iranian newspaper after a few moments. He walks to Sassan and Nazanine and shows them the front page of the newspaper, they look at the paper inquisitively.

A picture showing the bloody bodies of a few people who have reportedly been killed in a clash with police in Tehran can be seen in the middle of the page. Sassan and Nazanine who seem quite shocked read the paper speedily.

GHAFUR: *"They killed all those bastards. They gave Mammad the Wolf a pretty good going over before they shot him. I heard that they actually stuck a batten up his rear end."*

SASSAN: *"When did you find out about this?"*

GHAFUR: *"Before I received this newspaper I heard it on the phone. This kind of news is spread quickly, it is heartening to those in the organization. Also our enemies who even imagine to hurt the organization think twice when they hear news like this. They would know that we are not kidding* around. *Any other way and the whole thing will fall apart. The order and the respect will be gone. Then we won't be able to do business. The export business will be affected and the whole thing will go to hell. This is our credo. This is the way the game is played. Even those who work for the organization must know that if they step over the line there will be consequences. There will be hell to pay. Examples must be set."*

He pauses for a moment

"Of course Mammad the Wolf and his gang were small potatoes, we have dealt with people much more notorious than him."

Sassan and Nazanine who seem slightly concerned listen closely. Nargess enters the room, she says something to Ghafur in Turkish and leaves.

GHAFUR:*Turns to Sassan and Nazanine*

"Mustafa is here to take care of your passports. I told him to wait for us in the living room. Whenever you are ready, let me know and we can go there together."

SASSAN: *Turns to Nazanine*

"We are ready now."

They all get up

GHAFUR: *"I will introduce you to him. He must look at you."*

They all follow Ghafur and leave the room and enter the living room. Mustafa is tall and has light brown hair, he is around 30. He gets up from his chair and shakes everyone's hands. He speaks to Ghafur in Turkish. Mustafa inquisitively looks at both Nazanine and Sassan. Sassan and Nazanine look at him in a rather puzzled manner. Ghafur is calmly standing next to them and looking at Mustafa.

GHAFUR: *"Let's all sit down"*

They all sit

"Mustafa is one of our own. We have full confidence in him. Your passports will be ready in a couple of days."

SASSAN: *He takes out his wallet and hands a few passport size pictures of Nazanine and himself to Ghafur.*

"Please pass these to Mustafa so that he can use them for our passports."

GHAFUR: *While smiling*

"These won't be at all necessary. Don't you worry. Mustafa knows what he is doing."

Sassan seems baffled, he places the pictures in his pocket. Mustafa shakes hands with everybody. Says 'goodbye' and leaves the room.

THE COURTROOM

SASSAN: *Continues with his story as Arash listens closely. Nazanine listens as she agrees and goes along with what Sassan is saying*

"Believe me Mr Vaziri, it didn't take Ghafur more than two days before he called us and handed us our passports with British visas already stamped in them. And he personally gave us a ride to Istanbul international airport. We bought tickets for the next available flight and flew to England."

ARASH: *Looks at Sassan in utter disbelief*

"You mean no-one at Istanbul airport realized that you were carrying fake passports?"

After a moment

"Maybe Ghafur had paid them off too?"

SASSAN: *"When did I ever say that we were carrying fake passports? We had authentic original passports."*

ARASH: *Seems puzzled*

"This could not be. It is impossible."

SASSAN: *Approaches Arash*

"Of course we found out about this later on when Ghafur told us the story in detail. You see, Mustafa has a photographic memory. That is why he was looking at us, ogling us in that way the first time we met."

"He is in charge of general maintenance in several hotels in Istanbul. He recorded our faces in his perfect memory. Then he found two passengers whose looks were very similar to us and had their passports stolen from the hotel they were staying at. Then he quickly had the passports delivered to us. Good old lady luck smiled upon us since both passports contained

British visas."

Arash who does not seem too happy with what he is hearing shakes his head in disapproval. Sassan realizes Arash's displeasure.

"Arash, we had no other choice. Had we been caught we would have been deported back to Iran and that would have been the end of us. We were trapped."

ARASH: *He is deliberating what he just heard as he continues to listen*

"Wow! Unbelievable. You didn't have any trouble at the airport in London?"

SASSAN: *"Not at all, we breezed through."*

Arash opens his briefcase again and takes out his notebook and jots something down. Sassan and Nazanine seem worried as they watch Arash write in his notebook.

SASSAN: *"Mr Vaziri, please believe me I have not relayed a word of what I just told you to a single other soul. There is nothing mentioned about this in our case file. Please keep this between ourselves and do not talk about this to anyone else. I beg of you."*

ARASH: *"Of course not. Where do you live at the moment?"*

SASSAN: *"In the Brixton area of London. In a hotel with other refugees."*

ARASH: *"How is your English? How much do you understand? Can you speak the language?"*

NAZANINE: *Sassan and Nazanine look at each other*

"To be honest, except for a few words, that we picked up while over here, we don't know much."

ARASH: *"That is not important. I will translate whatever is said in the court that concerns you. Also whatever the Home Office barrister will ask. I will also interpret anything that your barrister might say on your behalf. I will also translate your answers for the court. You just listen carefully and answer the question that you are asked. You are absolutely not allowed to directly ask the judge any questions. You are also not allowed to speak until spoken to. Your answers must be short and to the point. Don't beat* *around the bush, speak clearly and give me a chance to translate what you said before continuing. Avoid using slang, local expressions etc. I will translate what you say word for word."*

He glances at Sassan and Nazanine.

"Have you met your solicitor yet?"

SASSAN: *"Yes, we briefly met him earlier with another interpreter present. It wasn't a very promising experience."*

ARASH: *"You are aware that your barrister's job is to defend your interests, however, the Home Office barristers job is quite the opposite. He will try to prove that all you say and the reasons you give for staying in this country are all baseless and untrue. He will ask the judge to deny your request for asylum."*

"He will do his best to convince the judge to deport you as soon as possible. That is why he is going to bombard you with a bunch of questions, all of which I shall translate for you word for word and will do the same when it comes to your answers."

NAZANINE: *"The Home Office barrister sounds like a nasty man. I hope he is ill and won't be able to make it today."*

ARASH: *Laughs "No my dear. He is neither trouble nor has he anything against you. This is what the poor man does for a living. You shouldn't vilify him. Just like your barrister who has never met you before, but will defend your right, he too will do his best for his client. He just happens to be on the opposite side. Furthermore, the court won't even go into session if he does not show up."*

SASSAN: *Looks Arash in the eye and speaks in a pleading tone*

"The past few years in Iran, we suffered very much. We finally managed to get here carrying a thousand dreams in our hearts. This court is our last chance. Please in case we say something that could hurt our case do not translate it for the court or the Home Office barrister. Please do not let all our hopes and dreams be shattered."

ARASH: *Gets annoyed*

"What are you talking about? Whatever you say I shall translate exactly. This is my legal duty. This is what I get paid for. The reason I am respected here is that I translate everything true to it's meaning without deviation."

Sassan looks at him, he tries to win him over.

SASSAN: "We were not telling tales or making up stories."

"As god is my witness we were not acting. What I meant was that maybe you could help us to properly convey our feelings to the judge. To help us get our case across. We were just rehearsing back there."

ARASH: *Seems to have understood what Sassan is saying*

"Maybe you didn't understand me correctly. Maybe I didn't explain myself properly. My dear sir, I will only translate what is said in the court, not what you told me earlier when we were outside the courtroom, neither what you are telling me now. I am not a Home Office informer."

NAZANINE: *Who seems reassured hearing Arash's words*

"We never accused you of such a thing, after all you are our fellow country man."

ARASH: "Please know that it is your right to ask for another translator if you wish. Please believe me, I wouldn't mind at all."

Nazanine and Sassan look at one another.

NAZANINE: "No, Arash, please, what are you saying? Whom can we find any better than yourself? At least you know some of what we have been through. I think there was a slight misunderstanding that you have managed to resolve."

ARASH: *Looks at his watch*

"Do you have any questions?"

NAZANINE: "I am sorry to ask you this question, but I am a little bit confused. You see Arash, our previous interpreter, who I shan't name, told us to explain everything very clearly and to the finest detail when addressing the judge. He told us to speak with feeling and even to shed a few tears to gain the judges sympathy."

ARASH: *Gets angry*

"He was very wrong in doing so dear lady. What do you think? Do you really believe that the judge is going to waste his day listening to made up scenarios and stories. His time is more valuable than that. He has to listen to several arguments and rule on several cases every day. Please do not pay too much attention to the rubbish that some people tell you. Just think, if asylum was to be granted to every Joe public who came into this court and shed a few tears, then the population of this country would be ten times greater than it is now. This is a country of laws, everything is in it's proper place, there is order. Even if you cry blood in front of the judge it won't make a difference. The judge will never allow emotions to cloud his logic or judgment. He follows the law and rules based on legal precedent. These judges are up to here, points to his neck, with sob stories and tragic tales. You need to produce documents to back-up what you say, to show you are genuine, not sobs and tears."

In the meantime, Jeff enters the room and turns to Arash.

JEFF: "The court will go into session in about an hour. Their barrister just called and told me that he will be here in about forty minutes. He wants you to wait for him right here, he needs to go over a few matters with his clients and wants you to translate for them."

ARASH: "Fine. No problem. I will wait right here."

"Jeff, you wouldn't know which judge is presiding today would you?"

JEFF: "Do you really want to know?"

ARASH: "Is it that bad?"

JEFF: "It is Mr. Peter Jones."

ARASH: "Oh my dear Lord" *Shakes his head.* "Hasn't he retired yet?"

JEFF: "Unfortunately not. I thought you would be pleased!"

ARASH: "Your barrister will be here in about forty minutes. He has asked us to wait here. He wishes to go over a few things with you before we go into court. I must also tell you, you have been assigned a pretty difficult and bad tempered judge. Make sure to give short and straight answers to *his questions. Not one word more not one word less, and remember sobs and tears don't do much for this old hand, he has seen it all before. The court is going to go into session with a slight delay."*

NAZANINE: *Is pretty scared. She turns to Arash.*

"For god's sake, if you feel that an answer we give is going to hurt our case, please do not translate it for the court. Translate it in a way that you feel is for the best. In a way that will help our case. These people don't understand Farsi anyway. God bless your soul Mr. Vaziri."

ARASH: *Becomes upset and slightly angry again.*

"Looks like you just don't get it do you? I have been working for this establishment with honesty and integrity for many years. I am respected here. They have put their trust in me. Most of the judges and barristers in this courthouse, even the clerks, down to the doormen and cleaners all know me. Should I have miss-translated every time someone said something that I felt would hurt their case, then I wouldn't enjoy the respect I enjoy today."

"I would have been thrown out of here a long time ago. What do you expect lady?"

He grabs his briefcase and puts his books and notebook inside it.

"That I risk losing my job to help your case? I will resign as your translator, I've had enough."

Sassan and Nazanine both get up and try to appease him.

SASSAN: *"Please forgive her. She didn't mean it the way it came across."*

NAZANINE: *Turns to Arash*

"Please sit down. I deeply apologise."

SASSAN: *Puts his hand on Arash's shoulder*

"Please forgive her. Have a glass of water, it will help calm you down. She didn't mean anything by it. She is not herself today. All the pressure and all that."

ARASH: *Sits back down and puts his briefcase back on the table. After a short silence.*

"I will return in a few minutes."

He leaves the room and leaves Sassan and Nazanine alone.

SASSAN: *"What an asshole! Who does he think he is? What a cold and insensitive snob. He doesn't have a sympathetic bone in his body. He seems to uphold these people's interest more passionately than they would themselves. Instead of giving us a little hope and reassurance he is confronting us. What's wrong with this guy?"*

NAZANINE: *"I think he is a Home Office informant. Did you notice how he quickly took out his notebook and began to jot down something when we were talking about Abdullah, Saleh, Ghafur and Mustafa?"*

SASSAN: *"I think you are right. He tells us that he is not a Home Office informant. If he isn't, why does he have to insist on not working for them? Why mention anything at all?"*

"We didn't accuse him of anything. He brought it up himself. Imagine, when we were in the hallway he was sitting on that bench behind us and listening to all we had to say. He was probably taking notes too."

NAZANINE: *"God help us with a translator like this. I don't think we have a chance with this spy and informer as our interpreter."*

They both look anxious and worried. Sassan impatiently paces around the room.

SASSAN: *Tries to reassure Nazanine*

"No big deal. If we are denied we can always ask for asylum in another European country. We might even be able to ask for asylum from the U.S. and go and visit your cousins there."

NAZANINE: *"How about telling Jeff to get us a different interpreter?"*
SASSAN: *"It's of no use. Arash is going to tell everything we said to the*

judge and the barrister anyhow. We must not create any new enemies in the dire situation that we are in. It is too late now."

In the meantime Arash enters the room and sits on a chair.

117

NAZANINE: *"Mr. Vaziri, should god forbid, the judge reject our case what is going to become of us?"*

ARASH: *Briefly pauses, takes a deep breath and begins to speak as he stares at the ceiling*

"From my experience, should you fail to produce the needed documents to prove your case and should the Home Office barrister instead succeed in convincing the court that your story is baseless and full of holes, tomorrow early in the morning the police will knock on your door, escort you to the airport, send you back to Iran and wish you farewell."

NAZANINE: *Is very frightened, mumbles something and speaks in a whimper*

"May the angels have mercy. Please help us."

Takes a deep breath

"God help us!"

SASSAN: *Arash is writing something*

"Have you ever witnessed such a case yourself?"

Arash doesn't get Sassan's meaning, he stares at him.

"I mean do they deport people without any warning? Without even giving them a chance to apply for asylum in another country?"

ARASH: *While contemplating what to say, is lying back in the chair with his hands behind his head and looking at the ceiling*

"Yes, I remember it well, it was many years ago when a young 20 year old Iranian Kurd was arrested for illegal entry. This young man whose name.....if I could recall.....was Rafat Shabani, applied for political asylum. One day Jeff whom you have met, called me at home and told me to be ready to interpret for this young man. Incidentally, Mr Peter Jones was presiding that day and the courtroom was full of journalists and reporters who had come to report the events of the day. There was interest in the case because a few Chinese nationals who were hiding in the same container as Rafat had died of thirst and hunger on the ship that was bringing them over."

THE COURTROOM

RAFAT'S TRIAL

Rafat a 20 year old tall young man of light complexion and sandy brown hair is standing in the witness box wearing a white shirt and brown trousers. There is a microphone placed in front of him. There is a jug of water and a glass to his left. The judge is sitting on his high-backed chair wearing a long robe and wig. A few large books and some case files can be seen at his side. Both Rafat's and the Home Office solicitor are on their feet. Arash is standing between the judge and Rafat and is ready to begin translation.

HOME OFFICE BARRISTER: *"Please tell the court which opposition group or organization you were a member of."*

Arash translates

RAFAT: *"I, my father, my brother and my cousins were all members of Kumala organization."*

Arash translates

HOME OFFICE BARRISTER: *"In what part of Iran did you live?"*

RAFAT: *"During summer, we lived in a small village called Chaveh near Shirin Bahareh on the footsteps of the Zagros Mountains near the Turkish border. During the winter season when heavy snow fell and the weather got to be unbearably cold we moved to Tehran and worked in Rashid Razzagi shoe works at the main bazaar."*

HOME OFFICE BARRISTER: *"Please tell the judge about this organization's ideology? Why did you decide to join this group and what did you do there?"*

Arash translates

RAFAT: *Deliberates for a moment*

"Kumalah is an organization that has been involved in an armed struggle against the revolutionary guard forces for the autonomy of Kurdistan for many years and not a week goes by without casualties on either side."

Arash translates

HOME OFFICE BARRISTER: *"You did not answer the question. Why did you become a member of this Marxist Leninist organization and what did you do there?"*

Arash translates

RAFAT: *Seems perplexed. He pauses briefly*

"Kumala is not a communist or Marxist organization. You have been misinformed. The dear Lord knows we all pray every day, we fast, we do not take our religious duties lightly. We all worship God almighty. We are definitely not communists."

Arash translates verbatim

ARASH: *Turns to Rafat*

"Now tell the court why you decided to join Kumalah and what role did you play in this organization."

RAFAT: *"Well that is obvious, I joined because my father, my brother and most men in my village were also members. Basically, what I did for them was to distribute pamphlets and stick posters around town."*

"What we were demanding was to be able to teach Kurdish in our schools, to have a Kurdish television and radio station. All these pamphlets said was democracy for Iran, self rule for Kurdistan"

Arash translates

HOME OFFICE BARRISTER: *"So you were not personally involved in taking up arms against the revolutionary guard?"*

RAFAT: *"No I wasn't. But had it been necessary, I certainly would not* *hesitate to do so."*

Arash translates

HOME OFFICE BARRISTER: *"Tell the court the name of Kumalas central committee members if you can remember."*

RAFAT: *"I can't remember any of those names. I don't know."*

HOME OFFICE BARRISTER: *"You don't seem to be familiar with this organizations credo and ideology. Neither could you give us the names of any members of this organization."*

He approaches Rafat, looks him directly in the eye, pauses shortly.

"Why then did you become a member of this organization? What was your incentive? What was your aim?"

RAFAT: *"My aim was to gain autonomy for Kurdistan and freedom for Iran."*

RAFAT'S BARRISTER: *Gets up and faces the judge*

"If your honour would allow Mr. Shabani to tell the court his account and explain how he fled Iran, I think everything would become clear."

Mr Jones nods his head in approval and turns to Arash.

"Ask him what happened and what incentive motivated him to bring this trouble upon himself and escape into Turkey through the Iranian border?"

Arash translates

RAFAT: *Deliberates for a while*

"It was early morning when I woke up to the sound of grenades and exploding shells."

A VILLAGE CALLED CHAVEH IN KURDISTAN

EARLY MORNING ONE SUMMER DAY

A small rustic courtyard house with several rooms. The doors to the rooms all open into the courtyard. Rafat and his brother Rashid who is 28 years old wearing Kurdish attire are deep asleep lying on a traditional hand woven rug. In the next room, Rafat's father Barzan and his wife, fifty year old Robabeh are sleeping on the floor. The sound of exploding shells and grenades can be heard from the outside. Barzan rushes to Rafat and Rashid and they hurriedly leave the room.

BARZAN: *Faces them*

"Looks like the revolutionary guards are launching an attack."

ROBABEH: *Looks at the sky*

"Dear Lord please have mercy."

Someone knocks on the door. Rashid opens the door. Azam, a 25 year old young man enters breathing heavily. Everyone gathers around him.

AZAM: *"The revolutionary guards have completely surrounded the hill. Several guards and Kumala fighters have already been killed. It shouldn't be long before they enter the village. There is too many of them. If you don't mind let Rashid come with us, we should take refuge in the mountains otherwise we will all be killed."*

BARZAN: *Turns to Rashid "Go with Azam"*

The fighting gets closer

ROBABEH: *Kisses Rashid's face. Rashid and Azam rush out*

"Please be careful son."

BARZAN: *To Rafat "Pile up all the posters and pamphlets, get some* kerosene and burn them. They must not see these. Hurry."

Turns to Robabeh

"I am going to step outside for a little while and see what the situation is like. I will be back soon."

ROBABEH: *"Shall I go with you?"*

BARZAN: *"No, where are you gonna go? Are you deaf? Can't you hear all the explosions? Can't you hear the sound of gunfire? You stay here."*

ROBABEH: *"Then come back quickly"*

Barzan leaves, Rafat goes into a storage shed where a few sacks of wheat and flour along with some water melons are stored and grabs two large cardboard boxes and drags them into the yard. He takes the bundles of posters and pamphlets and piles them on top of one another.

RAFAT: *"Mother, would you get me the bottle of kerosene and some matches?"*

Robabeh brings him the kerosene and a box of matches and hands them to him. Rafat pours some kerosene over the pamphlets and lights a match. The paper starts to burn.

ROBABEH: *"Be careful, don't burn yourself. May god curse them all"*

RAFAT: *"Don't worry. It will be alright."*

The pile is ablaze. Rafat pokes the pile with a stick. Half burnt pieces of paper rise up into the air and sway back down to the ground. The sun is just beginning to rise.

BARZAN: *Is moaning and groaning as he enters the house*

"I was shot."

ROBABEH: *"Oh my god....."*

Robabeh and Rafat go toward Barzan. Barzan closes the door behind him. Rafat and Robabeh begin to sob loudly as they help Barzan into the room and help him lie on a mattress.

ROBABEH: *"Oh my god, he is bleeding badly."*

BARZAN: *Indicates to Rafat to go closer, as he moans in pain. Rafat approaches and sits next to him on the floor*

"Listen carefully my son. Take all the money in that box and get away from here as fast as you can and save your life. It's only one or two kilometres to the border. Use the Laleh pass, get yourself to Turkey and through any means possible try to get to England and ask for asylum like your cousins Bakhshali and Mozzafar. Tell them that you are a member of Kurdish Kumala and that your life will be in danger if you return. Just like Bakhshali and Mozzafar, tell them that you will be executed, if you return to Iran. They will definitely give you refuge and help you out. I don't think that I will be around for much longer. Try and send some money for your mother every month like your cousins."

The sound of gunfire gets louder, Robabeh begins to sob.

RAFAT: *"father, I couldn't leave you like this. Who is going to take care of you and mother?"*

BARZAN: *He is moaning and now can be barely heard*

"We are too old now. We are at the end of our lives. They won't have any use for us. They are after the young men. Go quickly before they get here. Go quickly my son. Me and your mother are worried for you. Go."

RAFAT: *Reluctantly does what his father asks*

"But father....."

ROBABEH: *"I wish I had been shot instead, you are bleeding heavily. Dear Lord, what am I to do? Let me get some cloth and place it on your wound."*

She gets up and leaves the room.

RAFAT: *Looks at his father*

"Are you asking me to leave you alone like this and go?"

He pauses for a moment

"What about Rashid? I must say goodbye to him."

BARZAN: *His voice is weak and can barely be heard, he has lost a lot of*

124

blood. He indicates with his hand for Rafat to go closer to him

"Listen my son, don't let your mother find out yet, but the revolutionary guards killed your brother, Rashid and Azam, they got caught in their machine gun fire."

As he takes his final breaths

"Son, please hurry before they break into the house. Go quickly, please go, go!."

Rafat gets up, he is very upset, he goes toward the box and quickly grabs the cash that is inside. Robabeh enters the room holding a piece of cloth and some antiseptic ointment. Rafat tearfully kisses his mother and father's hands and leaves.

THE COURTROOM

RAFAT'S TRIAL

THE JUDGE: *Turns to the Home Office barrister*

"Do you have any questions for Mr. Rafat?"

HOME OFFICE BARRISTER: *Gets up as he is quickly jotting something down*

"Rafat answered all my questions. I will fully discuss this later. I do not have any further questions at the moment, your Honour."

He sits at the judges gesture. Arash translates.

RAFAT'S BARRISTER: *Pours some water into a glass and takes a sip*

"Please explain in full as to how you managed to get onto British soil."

Arash translates

RAFAT: *"I met a Turkish Kurd, called Shams in Amsterdam. He introduced me to a fellow called Nosrat who worked at the sea port. At first he was unwilling to help me since I didn't have enough money. Sham's father who himself was a Kurdish fighter had heard about my brother and my father interfered on my behalf and spoke to Nosrat."*

"He managed to talk his price down quite a bit. He gave him a few dollars and managed to persuade him to help me. Nosrat who was a crane operator told me not to bring anything along except for a little food and a few bottles of water. He told Sham's who understood his language very well that he was going to put us in a metal container. He told Shams that he would lift the container, and we would be at the very top so that we would be able to get enough air. He said that he would drill many holes into the container to allow enough air inside. He promised that we wouldn't have

126

to be in there more than three days. He also had told Shams that once we reach England, someone would get us out of the container and drive us to London. I was to meet Shams near the port at 12:30 midnight."

Arash translates

PORTSIDE PARKING LOT – AMSTERDAM

12:30 MIDNIGHT

Shams is a 20 year old young man wearing a zipped up parka and black trousers. Rafat is wearing a grey suit and is standing by the side of the road inside an empty parking lot. Rafat is nervous, the street is dark and deserted. Light rain is falling, every now and then a car passes by. In the meantime, a pick-up truck pulls into the parking lot and stops. He flashes his headlights at Shams and Rafat and then turns his lights off. Shams and Rafat run toward the pick-up truck. Two Chinese men, a Chinese woman and a 12 year old boy have already reached the pick-up before they get there. Nosrat pushes the tarp that is covering the back of the truck partly aside. He rearranges some boxes that are inside the back of the pick-up. He first indicates to the Chinese, they get in and sit on the floor of the pick-up. Shams and Rafat embrace one another. Rafat wipes off his tears and immediately gets inside the truck. The driver puts the tarp back on and hides the two Chinese men and the Chinese woman and boy who accompany them beneath it. He attaches the ropes to the hooks around the truck.

Nosrat starts the pick-up and drives away. Shams is standing in the parking lot all alone under the rain and is staring at the pick-up truck as it pulls away. The truck goes toward the gate and stops right outside. Nosrat gets out and exchanges pleasantries with the gate keepers. They look as if they know each other well. The gate keepers open the large iron door. The pick-up enters the port area and begins to make it's way between the rows and columns of containers that are neatly stacked in the port area. He looks in the rear view mirror and suddenly turns his lights off and makes an immediate left turn. He continues forward in the dark. He stops in the middle of a row of containers. He quickly gets out of the pick-

up and opens the door to a container. He removes the tarp from the back and everyone gets out and follows Nosrat into the container. Nosrat turns on his torch. There is an empty space at the back of the container. It is only about a metre wide and as long as the container. Everyone squeezes into this tight space. They are each holding a plastic bag and a small knapsack. Nosrat quickly replaces the boxes that had been removed to open a path to the back of the container. He looks outside and then closes the doors to the container and leaves.

THE COURTROOM

RAFAT'S TRIAL

Rafat has fallen silent. He is unable to continue. The journalists and reporters are eagerly waiting for Rafat to tell the rest of the story. The reporters who were until then hurriedly taking notes begin to chat amongst each other. The judge brings down the gavel and demands silence. Rafat's barrister turns to him as he asks Arash to translate.

RAFAT'S BARRISTER: *"You must explain to the court as to exactly what transpired in that container during the fourteen days and as to how only you and the 12 year old boy managed to survive? What befell those helpless Chinese people. How did they die?"*

Arash quickly translates. But Rafat is unable to speak, tears roll down his face. He wipes off his tears using his hand. Everyone is eagerly awaiting the rest of the story. At the judges gesture Arash approaches Rafat and encourages him to continue.

ARASH: *"Have a glass of water, try and get a hold of yourself, then try to remember and recall everything from the moment you got into the container until the time you reached Southampton."*

"Fully describe everything to the judge. Hopefully your story will help your case."

RAFAT: *Looks at Arash and is persuaded to continue*

"As Nosrat had promised, he lifted and placed the container that we were in on top of the rest so that a little light and some air could reach us through the holes that he had drilled on top and around the container. The Chinese all sat on one side of the tight space and I sat on the other side. We never said anything to each other since we didn't speak one another's language.

On the third day that we were all expecting to reach England, the ship suddenly stopped in the middle of the sea and dropped anchor."

Arash translates

RAFAT'S BARRISTER: *"How do you know that the ship stopped and dropped anchor?"*

RAFAT: *"We couldn't feel the vibration from the ship's engines anymore. Nor could we hear it. Also, one of the Chinese fellows and I both stood on top of one of the boxes and looked outside through one of the holes. All we could see around us was the open sea, no sign of land anywhere. Only a few large ships could be seen in the distance. The sea was calm. The Chinese men were very impatient and agitated. They kept looking through the holes. We were all waiting for the ship to move again. But it didn't seem to want to move at all. The next day a severe storm hit and the ship rocked violently from side to side."*

Rafat has become very emotional as he speaks, Arash continues to speedily translate. The reporters continue to take notes. Everyone in the courtroom has their eyes intently fixed on Arash.

INSIDE THE CONTAINER – AT SEA

MORNING

The sound of the howling wind can be heard, the container is being rocked from side to side in the rough sea. A faint light reaches the inside of the container through the holes. The Chinese have huddled together at one end and Rafat is sitting alone at the other end of the container. Suddenly several large heavy boxes fall on top of the Chinese. They begin to shout and moan and mutter something in Chinese. Rafat while trying to keep his balance quickly reaches them and helps one of the Chinese men remove the box off the top of the rest. Some of the Chinese have been injured and are bleeding. They pull the 12 year old who seems uninjured away as his mother has passed out on the floor. Her head is bleeding profusely. They all begin to scream in horror. Rafat finds a metal rod and begins to bang it on the container wall. A Chinese man also takes a piece of metal and begins to bang it on the container. No-one comes to their rescue. They sit back down tired and helpless. Rafat squats in the corner and stares at the Chinese who have gathered around the body of the poor woman and are weeping and crying.

THE COURTROOM

RAFAT'S TRIAL

RAFAT'S BARRISTER: *He looks into the case file, turns to Rafat*

"Did only Ms. Chin Chang, the boy's mother die at that time?"

Arash translates

RAFAT: *"Yes"*

RAFAT'S BARRISTER: *"Please then explain to the court as to how the other two Chinese men, Lee Chang and Nay Chang lost their lives."*

Arash translates

RAFAT: *Is staring into the distance*

"After we removed the Chinese woman's body and placed it between the boxes at the front of the container, we spent many nights and days desperately and impatiently waiting for the ship to start to move again. Every day, with all the little strength that we had left, we used to bang on the container walls in the hope that someone might hear us, but no-one ever came."

He continues after a long pause.

"One day the sun came out. It was a very hot day. The Chinese had no water left."

"The boy kept crying. Kept asking for water and sucking on the plastic water bottles."

Rafat falls silent for a while and then continues

"My grandfather always used to say when travelling, always carry more water than you do food. He used to say one could die from thirst much

133

faster than one can from hunger. I had a few extra bottles of water with me. I hid them in one of the boxes so that the Chinese wouldn't find out about them."

INSIDE THE CONTAINER

HIGH NOON – A SWELTERING DAY

The sun's rays enter the container through the drilled holes in the roof. The young Chinese boy who is desperately thirsty and parched sucks on a now empty water bottle and tries to suck the last drop as he quietly whimpers. The two Chinese men who are now hopelessly frail and weak helplessly look at the boy. Rafat who is restless from the heat looks on. After a short while he sticks his hand into one of the boxes nearby, takes a plastic water bottle out and offers it to the young boy. The boy quickly gulps down some water and hands the bottle back to Rafat. The now gravely ill Chinese men look on with an appreciative smile but do not ask for any water. A few moments on, Rafat feeling rather guilty, takes out the water bottle and offers it to the Chinese men. They both refuse. One of the men puts the boy's hand in Rafat's and asks him to look after him. Rafat who is perplexed at the Chinese men's behaviour hesitates briefly and again offers them some water. They do not accept. Rafat takes the boys hand and takes him to the other side of the container.

THE COURTROOM

RAFAT'S TRIAL

RAFAT: *"That same night, both Chinese men died of thirst. They just lay there, the sun's rays shone through the holes and lit their faces in the morning. They looked as if they were in a deep sleep."*

Arash translates, there is a commotion in the courtroom

HOME OFFICE BARRISTER: *Asks the judge for permission to speak. The judge approves.*

"At the time that the two Chinese men died of thirst, how many bottles of water did you have left?"

RAFAT: *"I think I still had three bottles left. Maybe three and a half."*

HOME OFFICE BARRISTER: *"Why then didn't you at least offer those poor souls one of the bottles so that they wouldn't die of thirst?"*

Arash translates

RAFAT: *"I did, but they would not accept. I suppose they knew that they were dying. They wanted me to share what was left with the boy so that at least he could survive, and that is what I did."*

Arash translates

RAFAT'S BARRISTER: *Get's up and asks the judge for permission to speak. The judge gestures him to go ahead.*

"Your Excellency, during the police questioning, the boy confirmed what Rafat is saying."

The judge looks at the case file in front of him and nods in approval as he gestures to the barrister to continue.

RAFAT*: "Two to three days later the water was gone. We were both lying on the floor of the container semi-conscious. Suddenly we heard noises outside. I felt as if the container was being lifted. When they placed the container back down, both I and the boy began to bang on the container walls with all the might we had left. We began to shout at the top of our lungs."*

CITY OF SOUTHAMPTON – PORTSIDE

THE CONTAINER TERMINAL

A large cargo ship has docked and is waiting. Many containers can be seen on it's deck. The cranes are off-loading the containers and neatly stacking them on the dock. A couple of workers nearby, wearing blue zipped up overalls and yellow luminescence safety vests, supervise the operation on the ground. One of them talks to the crane operator on a walkie-talkie and is directing him where to place each container. In the meantime the banging sound from the container attracts the attention of one of the workers. The walkie-talkie is very loud. The workers suddenly realises he can hear noises coming from one of the containers.

FIRST WORKER: *"Turn that bloody thing down. I can hear some noise coming from this container".*

SECOND WORKER: *Turns off his two-way radio. They both approach the container and put their ears to the container wall.*

"My god, there is someone in there. He is screaming something, can you hear it?"

FIRST WORKER: *"Yes, yes I can hear it. You are right."*

They quickly open the container door.

THE COURTROOM

RAFAT'S TRIAL

The journalists and reporters and everyone else in the courtroom are frozen on their seats and intently listening to Arash who seems affected and emotional.

RAFAT'S BARRISTER: *Turns to the judge*

"Your Excellency, what is evident and obvious from this young man's testimony is that should this court, that is indeed his last chance, reject my client's request for asylum, he will without a doubt be prosecuted and possibly put to death by the Iranian authorities due to his membership in the Kumala organization. This young man has been through hell and high water trying to get to this free country and as we all just heard, like those two poor Chinese men, he almost lost his life in doing so. I respectfully ask your Excellency to approve this young man's request for asylum."

There is silence. The judge indicates to Rafat's barrister to sit down.

THE HOME OFFICE BARRISTER: *Gets off his seat and clears his throat.*

"Your Excellency, what the court must consider is the fact that this person's claims of membership in the Marxist and terrorist Kumala organization are all baseless and false. How is it possible for a person who is a member of an organization not to know the group's credo and ideology? Rafat claims that Kumala is not a communist organization. He claims that the members pray and fast. He cannot even come up with the names of any of the members of the central committee. Any of the leaders. The story about how his father and brothers got killed is just that, a story. It's all lies. Nothing has been reported in the papers for the period he is describing.

He has been coached to say all of this. This whole thing is made up, fantasy."

Arash translates for Rafat.

RAFAT: *While sobbing*

"I swear to god, I am not lying, on that terrible day, both my father Barzan and my brother Rashid were shot and killed."

THE JUDGE: *Turns to Arash*

"Ask him if he can produce any documents or witnesses that can confirm his membership in the group."

Arash translates

RAFAT: *"God knows I have no-one here, I don't know anybody. I swear on the Qoran."*

THE JUDGE: *Looks at his notes*

"In your testimony you mentioned your cousins Bakhshali and Mozzafar live in England. Don't you have their address or phone number?"

RAFAT: *"No sir, all I know is that they live somewhere in England."*

The judge indicates to the Home Office barrister to continue.

HOME OFFICE BARRISTER: *"What is certain is that Rafat's father Barzan encouraged him to seek a better life and living conditions in this country and to get here through any illegal means. He has been coached to claim that he is a member of the Kumala Organization so that he can obtain political asylum and enjoy the associated benefits. At the same time he has been told to work here illegally and send money to support his family at home as do his cousins. This person's life is not at all in danger should he return to Iran. I am not even so sure that he is of Kurdish origin or that he actually comes from Kurdistan."*

He turns to the judge.

"If I may your honour, I would like to ask Mr. Vaziri, Rafat's translator a question." *The judge allows the question.*

"I would like you to tell the court in which language Rafat spoke. Kurdish

or Farsi?"

ARASH*: "Farsi of course. I do not speak Kurdish."*

HOME OFFICE BARRISTER*: "How was his accent? I mean, did he speak with a Kurdish accent?"*

ARASH*: "Not at all. He speaks Farsi very well. Just like a born Farsi speaker. Without an accent."*

HOME OFFICE BARRISTER*: "Thank you sir, I have no further questions."*

He turns to the judge. "I must add your Excellency, this person was absolutely uncooperative and refused to provide the police with information regarding Sham's and Sham's father who helped him illegally enter this country."

Arash translates.

RAFAT*: "Sham's and his father were both kind and generous to me. I will never allow myself to get them in trouble. This would be against my beliefs. We Kurds don't bite the hand that feeds us. We never forget a kindness."*

Arash translates.

HOME OFFICE BARRISTER*: "What is clear and self evident is that Rafat, just like the Chinese who accompanied him have gone through a lot of trouble to reach this country for mainly economic reasons, to use the social and economic benefits this country offers. Should your honour approve this young man's request, the media gathered here will say that Britain offers asylum to anyone who takes the trouble of getting there. Then the next thing you know, we will have container loads of people from Africa, China and the Middle East trying to reach our shores. We would only be encouraging similar tragedies and witnessing more and more people losing their lives, as did the Chinese, trying to get here. Rafat broke the law trying to come to this country. We must not agree with his request to gain asylum here as this would encourage thousands of others to follow suit. I ask your honour to deny this law breaking immigrant's request for asylum and to deport him to his country forth with. This person's life is not at all threatened in his home country. Ironically, he has not broke any laws* *where he comes from."*

Arash translates and Rafat begins to speak.

THE JUDGE: *Facing Arash*

"What is he saying?"

RAFAT: *"I beg your Excellency to forgive me for breaking the law. I had no choice. Please allow me to remain in this country. I promise you that I will never do anything illegal ever again. If you deport me back to the Islamic Republic today, they will arrest me the moment I step off the plane and immediately execute me. Just as they have so many other Kurds."*

Arash translates.

WAITING ROOM AT THE COURTHOUSE

ARASH: *"To make the story short, the judge did not agree to his request for political asylum and ordered him deported. A couple of days later I saw him on the news being dragged onto the plane by two policemen. He was sent back to Iran. A few weeks later, I read in a newspaper that he was arrested and executed, accused of being involved in an armed struggle against the Islamic Republic. He was declared to be an infidel which carries the death penalty in Iran as you well know."*

NAZANINE: *Looking sad as she listens to Arash. She wipes her tears.*

"Couldn't you do anything for him? You must feel pretty guilty?"

ARASH: *"What could I do for him? It is the judge who decides not I. All I do is translate that's all. Why should I feel guilty? I didn't do anything wrong. I am not responsible for the deeds of Rafat and others like him. They make their own decisions."*

There is silence.

SASSAN: *"Have you ever travelled back to Iran since you settled here in England?"*

ARASH: *"Yes, actually only last year I paid a visit along with my wife who is English."*

SASSAN: *"They didn't give you any trouble? Didn't they ask you what you did here?"*

ARASH: *"Not at all. Everyone was very respectful and kind. Despite the fact that I had mentioned exactly what I do in the passport application form."*

NAZANINE: *"What do you think about Iran?"*

ARASH: *"Well to be honest, both me and my wife had a great time over there. My wife never expected Tehran to be such a modern, clean and beautiful city. They have really done a good job. Tehran looks just like any large and well run European city. Specially with the wide modern highways they have recently built. Also the beautifully landscaped parks and the newly established and efficient underground network. We really enjoyed our visit. Just think how far we have fared when it comes to medicine and industry. Iran recently launched a satellite into orbit. You must have surely heard, Iranian scientists managed to send some live creatures into space just a few weeks ago. Some great achievements have been made. We were both happy to have witnessed all this progress."*

NAZANINE: *"How come then, as you well know, thousands of Iranians flee their country every year and ask for asylum from European countries?*

Arash cuts her off.

ARASH: *"I am not saying that all is perfect in Iran. There are obviously problems and issues to be dealt with. These things could occur in any country. Some are worse and some are better."*

SASSAN: *Looks at Arash in amazement*

"You only stayed there for one or two weeks. You only touched the surface. So what if the regime managed to shoot a few earthworms and frogs into space?

"What's this going to do for the millions of poor and destitute Iranians who can hardly feed their families? Take it from me, had you spent a little longer time there you would realize that the whole country is up to it's neck in corruption, desperation and crime. I spent a lifetime in that country. The country has been driven to the edge of destruction. You can buy everyone with money. Judges, the police, government officials, they are all on the take. You can do anything you want as long as you have money and connections. My dear Arash, unemployment and inflation have made it unbearable for people to live a decent life. You have to work like a dog from dawn till dusk just to be able to pay your rent. No-one dares to speak. Should you utter the slightest criticism, you will be accused of being an anti-revolutionary and thrown into jail. You will be finished."

He whispers into Arash's ear.

"Prostitution and drug use are everywhere. Iranian girls are sold in the Gulf countries. Sold into prostitution. All you have seen is probably a few nicely kept streets and parks in the affluent northern section of Tehran. You must not judge the whole country by that. It would not be fair."

ARASH: *Angrily cuts him off*

"It is rather interesting to see someone like you preach about corruption, lawlessness and prostitution."

He pauses briefly

"The same goes on in many European countries although probably to a different extent. For example some of the things, like adultery, that are considered to be capital crimes in Islamic countries, are not even considered to be an offence in Europe."

"Here in this country, the previous Prime Minister, Mr John Major, whom you have probably heard of, had an affair with one of the ministers in his cabinet. Her name was Edwina Curry. What is interesting is that she confessed to the affair in her book. Nobody could even touch them. They had not broken the law."

Sassan does not seem at all interested or impressed with what Arash is saying. He stares at the ceiling indifferently. Arash notices Sassan's lack of interest but goes on regardless.

ARASH: "We are not getting anywhere. This is a pointless discussion. There isn't much time left anyway. You had better get ready. I am going to find your barrister and bring him to you."

Arash leaves the waiting room.

SASSAN: *Looks at Nazanine*

"What a heartless piece of crap. Did you notice? He didn't show an inkling of despair or remorse when he was speaking about poor Rafat and the way he was executed. I was closely watching him."

NAZANINE: "You never know, he might have ratted on Rafat to the Islamic Republic regime himself! And given them a copy of his case file."

SASSAN: *He nods in agreement*

"Do you mean that he is an informant for the Islamic Republic?"

Nazanine nods.

"Do you mean that he is an information ministry secret agent? Could be! The bastard that I saw could be both working for the Home Office and the ministry of intelligence. He gets paid from both sides. Anything is possible with this weasel."

NAZANINE: *Nazanine who is deliberating what Sassan just said seems worried and scared.*

"May the dear lord help us both. What are we going to do Sassan? If he passes our case file along to the Islamic Republic, with everything that we said and our signed confessions, they will have us stoned to death immediately. There won't even be a trial! Believe me Sassan attending this asylum hearing doesn't even bother me anymore. What really worries me is, god forbid, to be tried in the Islamic Republic's medieval courts."

As she wipes off her tears.

"Early in the morning they will send a few policemen after us and take us to the airport. God help us."

SASSAN: *Tries to calm her down*

"There is still hope sweetheart. My dear, we must not lose hope. The court hasn't even gone into session yet. No-one knows what's going to happen."

NAZANINE: "I wish you hadn't argued with him that way, not now. This guy can hurt us. What use was it? All you did was to upset him."

She is quietly whimpering. Sassan appears remorseful at what he has done.

"There isn't a single person here looking after our interests. Our supposed barrister seems to be an idiot. No-one knows where the hell he has gone? He should at least give us a few pointers before the court goes into session. He doesn't give a shit whether or not we are granted asylum.

SASSAN: *Sassan puts his hand around Nazanine's shoulders.*

"Don't worry my dear."

"The dear Lord will never close all the doors to his children."

In the meantime Arash enters the room accompanying James, their barrister. James is carrying a thick file and a large book.

JAMES: *Starts to speak in English. Arash translates*

"There isn't much time left. The Home Office barrister has arrived. He is waiting in court. Please follow me, I will briefly explain a few things to you."

They leave the room together and enter the courtroom.

THE COURTROOM

SASSAN AND NAZANINE'S TRIAL

The Home Office barrister, like the Defence Attorney, is wearing a white wig and long black robe. He is standing behind a table on the left side of the courtroom. The court stenographer is sitting behind a typing machine one row ahead of him near the judge. They all gather near the corner at the right side of the court. The Defence Barrister begins to speak with Arash.

ARASH: *Translates*

"Your barrister just wants to remind you of a couple of things. Firstly, to listen to the questions you are asked very carefully and to answer the question correctly. Do not volunteer information. Answer only the question. Secondly, do not speak unless you are spoken to."

SASSAN: *"That's all?"*

He seems at a loss.

ARASH: *"Yes, that's all."*

SASSAN: *He indicates to Nazanine and they both approach Arash.*

"Mr. Vaziri, both Nazanine and I would like to apologize for arguing with you and making you upset. We hope that you can find it in your heart to forgive us. Anyway, we hope you won't harbour any hard feelings."

ARASH: *"Not at all. Not in the least."*

At the indication of the Defence Barrister...

"Please sit down. The judge will be here soon."

The Home Office barrister signals to Arash with his hand. Arash walks towards him and shakes his hand. *It seems as if they have known each other for years. They begin to chat. They laugh and seem happy. Sassan and Nazanine look on apprehensively. Their distrust and disgust of Arash is fanned at seeing him being so friendly with the enemy.*

NAZANINE: *She whispers into Sassan's ear*

"Look how lovey-dovey they are. Looks like they are talking about us. Look at how they are laughing at us."

ARASH: *Stops talking to the Home Office barrister, approaches Nazanine and Sassan and says...*

"The gentleman I was just speaking to is the barrister representing the Home Office."

SASSAN: *"O.K. Mr Vaziri. We guessed he might be! We thought that ourselves."*

In the meantime, the judge is announced. Everyone in the courtroom stands. The judge enters the courtroom, walks towards his high backed chair and sits down. He signals a hand gesture to everyone in the courtroom to sit down. The judge opens a file that he carried with him. There is absolute silence. The judge slowly turns the pages and takes a few notes. Nazanine and Sassan look pale. They anxiously stare at the judge. With a signal from the judge, the Home Office barrister asks Arash to tell Nazanine to step up to the witness stand. Nazanine immediately walks up to the stand and waits there. The Home Office barrister and the Defence attorney talk to each other and then consult the judge.

Sassan's eyes are fixed on the Home Office barrister who has a pile of books and files scattered in front of him. Sassan looks aloof. He seems lost in his thoughts and dreams. He has lost hope of obtaining an English visa and instead is mulling his and Nazanine's defence in the Iranian courts. He is peering at the barristers and the judge, who are wearing black robes like the Mullahs in Iran. Instead of turbans – he thinks to himself – they are wearing white wigs.

SASSAN: *"Look at these people for god sake. They look just like our own Mullahs. Specially this judge with his beard and long black robe. He could* *double for one of our own Sharia judges. Look at their robes. Looks like they are all made of the same cloth, they are all black. They seem to share the same tailor. They look like penguins from the north pole. If that judge takes off his stupid wig and instead wraps a turban around his fat head, he would look just like Ayatollah Zareh, the Sharia judge for Koohpayeh."*

He looks at Arash.

"We should get this dumb bastard a robe too. He looks just like one of our own lousy and useless Mullah's. His job suits him too. Kissing these people's backsides day in and day out. It doesn't make a damn difference to him whose arse he kisses, whether be it these English Ayatollah's or the Mullah's back home. He should be promoted from translating to being the barrister for the Home Office. He should be promoted from being a bastard to being a real bastard."

An imaginary courtroom begins to take shape in Sassan's mind. Arash is wearing a long black robe and is standing next to the judge. The judge is wearing a huge white turban and sitting on a high-backed chair.

"I won't let this piece of shit get his way. I will kick his arse first. I will show him for what he really is right here in this courtroom. Just wait until it is my turn to speak. I know what I have to say. He wants to destroy our lives but I won't let him. I will disgrace him for all to see.

"Are you laughing at me you asshole. You don't know the half of it. I know these Sharia judges much better than you."

He gets off his seat, walks towards the judge and greets him, pours himself a glass of water, looks at Nazanine who is wearing a black veil, clears his throat and takes a deep breath.

SASSAN: *"My name is Sassan. My surname is Yazdani. I was born in April, 1966. I was born in Khorramabad in the province of Luristan. We live in the Nasiabad neighbourhood of Tehran."*

He faces the judge. What he sees is a fat bearded Mullah wearing a long black robe and sitting on a high-backed chair instead of the English judge. Jeff is standing at the side like a revolutionary guard and Nazanine is staring at him in her black chador.

"Haj Agha, I beg of you not to pay any attention to anything that this person has to say."

He points to Arash

"He is a very dubious fellow! He has been working for the British Home Office under the cover of translator for many years but in reality he is their informer, he is a spy!"

"This case file and the reports you find in it were all made up. They are products of his sick and devious imagination. He might at the present pretend to be working for your ministry of intelligence, but in reality he is trained and works for the British. Haj Agha I wish you knew how passionately he looks after their interests. He speaks of their judiciary system with great fondness and pride. As if justice is a foreign word to us. He makes it look as if god's rule hasn't reached us and lawlessness prevails. He kept saying the praise of English judges. He said that they won't rule unless there was ample evidence and documented proof. Haj Agha, just imagine what a poor innocent soul who can't provide the necessary documents, evidence or witnesses is going to go through. This person is devoid of any decency or fairness. He has made up false and baseless dossiers for many people and unjustly sent them to their doom."

He has left the witness stand and is pacing about the court like a prosecutor and trying Arash.

"He himself described to us as to how he made up a false dossier for poor Rafat."

He faces the judge.

"Haj Agha, poor Rafat would say one thing and this cruel animal would translate something else. All poor Rafat was after, was to be able to stay in this country. All he wanted was a peaceful life."

Sassan has become excited as he tries to arouse the judges emotions.

"O.K. maybe Rafat had hoped to fulfil his life's dreams and hopes on this island."

He speaks slowly and clearly.

"Maybe find a job and send some money home to help his poor family so that they won't be a burden upon the Islamic Republic."

He speaks loudly in an angry and resentful tone.

"But this fiend destroyed it all." *He calms down a bit and faces the judge.*

"Out of ignorance and desperation, he made some false claims, he had thought that if he made the court believe that he used to be a member of Kumala, he would be granted political asylum."

He bitterly approaches Arash and points his finger at him.

"You heartless fiend, have you no conscience? He was your fellow countryman! You claim to have worked for this establishment for many years. You say that all these judges know you on a first name basis. Haven't you yet learned how to translate so that these poor souls will be able to gain asylum and permanent residence?"

He points to Arash again.

"He claims that most of these asylum seekers come to this country for economic reasons. Free housing, free food, free medicine."

He angrily approaches Arash and looks at him.

"You miserable bastard. It's not your money. It's no skin off your nose if the British government is helping these desperate refugees? Haj Agha, the Home Office has coached this person to translate in a manner that none of these people will ever be granted asylum."

Takes a deep breath and paces about.

"Haj Agha, I presume that the Home Office rewards him with a commission every time he manages to get someone deported. Bravo Mr. Bravo. Well done. Very well done."

He comes forward and looks at Arash with resentment. Arash calmly smiles at him.

"He himself described to me how poor Rafat spent two terrible weeks in that damned container all thirsty and famished."

"Hiding in that metal box just to reach this island of hope, just to be able to

have a decent life. To reach and fulfil his hopes and dreams."

He points to Arash again as he turns to the judge.

"This liar turned the court's decision by mis-translating what was said and prevented him from being able to obtain a refugee visa and permanent residence."

He walks to Arash and asks in a despondent tone

"Why? Why did you make up that false and baseless dossier and give it to this honourable judge? So what if Rafat had made a false claim?"

With a bit of sarcasm

"That sure I am, one of the feared members of Kumala, I am going to wage war against the Islamic Regime."

Turns to Arash.

"That poor young soul had not even seen a weapon all his life."

Looks at Arash again.

"If Rafat really meant to join an armed struggle against the regime, why would he come here for food? You yourself have seen how so many people trying to gain asylum would go to any means claiming to have become Christians, Bahais."

Turns to the judge.

"The fellow is a Seyyed, his ancestry goes all the way back to the prophet himself and just to gain asylum, he claims to have become a Zoroastrian."

Turns to Arash.

"You yourself said that it is all a bunch of made up lies."

Arash has his head down and is looking at the ground.

"Look at me you traitor! This Haj Agha is a very fair and just judge. He is renowned all across Iran. The death sentences he issued for Rafat and others like him were based on the baseless dossier that you put together for Rafat and others. Their unfairly shed blood is on your hands. Not this cherished judge, not this holy man."

153

Sassan looks at the judge. He seemed content to have gained the judges confidence. He paces toward Nazanine who is wearing a black veil and smiles at her as if he is trying to console her. He walks back to the judge and tries to attract his attention, he points to his wife.

SASSAN: *"Haj Agha! My wife Nazanine is a true angel, a true human being, a kind and excellent home maker, believe me, not once have I come home without dinner being ready. She always prepares breakfast early in the morning before I get up. My clothes are always clean and neatly pressed and stacked in the cupboard. Haj Agha, you must promise to come to our home for some tea and biscuits. You could come to our home and see for yourself how tidy and well kept it is. She always has fresh flowers around."*

He points to Nazanine.

"This wife of mine is also an exceptional host. As you have been informed."

The judge glances at the case file as he listens to Sassan.

"I have two jobs. During the day I teach at an elementary school and in the evenings I work with my taxi, sometimes up to a couple of hours past midnight."

Faces the judge.

"As god is my witness, not once did I come home and not find her waiting up for me."

He points to Nazanine.

"Haj Agha, if it wasn't for her, there is no way on earth that I could work for 17-18 hours a day and manage our livelihood. This woman also works at the Shafa Public Hospital part-time as an auxiliary nurse."

Turns to the judge.

"Haj Agha, do you know what she did there?"

The judge looks at the case file.

"She is a real angel your honour. After she did her housework she used to go to Shafa Hospital at the intersection of Edalat and Rasekh streets and

look after the gravely ill patients whom the doctors had given up hope for. She washed and bathed them."

He approaches the judge.

"She would even wash their bottoms and change their sheets. She would comb their hair. I will never forget one afternoon when I went to Shafa Hospital to see what she did there.

SHAFA HOSPITAL

3:30PM

Sassan wearing a suit is standing outside Shafa Hospital and looking at the sign, he proceeds towards the front door and enters the hallway. He could see several nurses wearing white uniforms and head scarf's walking around. A few patients are being pushed around on wheel chairs and carried about on stretchers. Sassan approaches the information desk. A young man in his late twenties is standing behind the desk. A large log book is in front of him.

SASSAN: *"Good morning Sir, I wanted to see my wife."*

YOUNG MAN: *"Good morning, is she a patient or does she work here?"*

SASSAN: *"No she isn't a patient, she works here."*

YOUNG MAN: *"Then please wait for a minute."*

The young man opens the door to the office in the back and in a short while returns with the head nurse who is a woman in her forties. She is wearing a white nurses uniform and a white head scarf.

HEAD NURSE: *With a smile*

"Good morning Sir, what is your wife's name?"

SASSAN: *"Nazanine Afshar"*

"My name is Sassan Yazdani"

HEAD NURSE: *"Hello Mr. Yazdani. I have heard alot about you from Nazanine, she speaks very well of you. I am the head nurse here. Did you want to see her?"*

SASSAN: *"Well, I just wanted to see what my wife does here. I hope you* *are happy with her work."*

HEAD NURSE: *"One hundred percent Mr Yazdani. If you wish to see her, I will take you to her."*

SASSAN: *"If it won't be any trouble. I wouldn't mind seeing what she does."*

HEAD NURSE: *Turns to Sassan*

"Then please follow me."

Sassan follows her.

"Mr Yazdani, your wife, god bless her kind heart, works in the Refah ward of the hospital. Dying and incurable patients for whom the doctors don't hold out any hope are brought to this ward. Patients who usually haven't long to live. They even stop their medicine. Even the regular nurses don't tend to them any longer, well they really don't have the time. They must devote their time to patients for whom there is hope of a cure. The patients in this ward are unconsciously lying on their bed most of the time. Everyone is just waiting for them to pass away. Your wife, Ms. Nazanine, looks after this type of patients and checks on them. She cleans them up, and changes their incontinence pants, changes their bed sheets, washes and baths them when needed and feeds and takes care of them. She basically does the tasks that nobody else in this hospital is really willing to perform."

In the meantime a nurse rolling a bed along the hallway attracts their attention. A dead patient is lying on the bed. He is covered with a white sheet. His hands are showing outside of the sheet.

"Look at this. This person has died. We see three or four of these every day."

SASSAN: *Sighs*

"Well, god rest their souls."

HEAD NURSE: *"I told Nazanine to clean up this poor old mother Sadiqeh. She is so weak she can hardly breathe anymore. I asked her to try and feed her some soup, to give her some water so that at least she won't* *pass away thirsty. Her room smelled so bad you could hardly stand it. I was even embarrassed to ask Nazanine to clean up in there but there was no choice. In a few months cancer gradually took over all her body, she doesn't have much longer to live."*

The head nurse stops near the room and turns to Sassan.

"Now, are you sure you would like to see what Nazanine does?"

SASSAN*: Reluctantly takes out his handkerchief and holds it in front of his nose*

"Yes I would like to know."

The head nurse slowly half opens the door. She glances inside and then quickly opens the door and walks to the middle of the room. Sassan follows her in. Mother Sadiqeh is an eighty two year old woman. She is wearing a white dress and sitting on the bed. Nazanine is feeding her soup as they warmly chat. The room seems very clean. The head nurse starts to speak.

HEAD NURSE*: "Here you are. Your wife is a real miracle worker."*

THE COURTROOM

SASSAN AND NAZANINE'S TRIAL

Haj Agha doesn't seem at all impressed with what Sassan had to say. He is reading the case file in front of him. He signals to Arash with his hand. Arash quickly goes to him. Sassan nervously looks on. Haj Agha points to and shows one of the pages to Arash. Arash looks at Sassan in a mocking way and whispers something into the judges ear and then goes back to his seat. He continues to look at Sassan in a ridiculing manner. There is silence. The judge looks at the case file and then writes something down. Sassan who is looking on is slightly set aback. He tries to attract the judges attention again.

SASSAN: *"Haj Agha, there is an issue I wanted to discuss and bring up in this courtroom. My dear and honourable Excellency, for someone who rules based on our Islamic and heavenly holy book, you shouldn't really pay much attention to this paid Home Office informant. This man makes things up."*

Haj Agha gives Sassan a look as he seems displeased with what he just said. He scratches his beard. Sassan is taken aback. The judge begins to look at the case file again. Arash quietly laughs at Sassan.

SASSAN: *Looks at Nazanine* *"Nazanine hasn't seen her cousins, Mohsen and Sepideh, for many years. They live in the United States. They are very well off. They have both managed to become doctors and have a good practice."* *Sassan feels slightly more confident as he suddenly thinks of his wife's cousins.*

"Haj Agha, to be honest, we really do not plan to stay in England. We were just hoping to gain residence so that we could stay until we have learnt English before we travel to America and apply for green cards. We

159

needed to put together a credible story Haj Agha."

There is silence. He approaches the judge and continues with a smile.

"Let it be known to you, my wife's cousin Sepideh just got engaged, those young souls are all alone, strangers in America. They haven't any family close by. Nazanine badly wanted to attend their wedding."

He gives Nazanine a kind and sympathetic look.

"Poor uncle Sadeq is not with us anymore."

Haj Agha seems angry at the mention of this name. He stands up. Arash quickly approaches him and points to a page in the case file. They both look at the page intently. Arash points to a paragraph on the page. Sassan looks on bedazzled and distraught. After a short while Arash returns to his seat looking victorious. The judge sits back on his chair and begins to read. Sassan tries to regain the initiative. He looks as if he has an idea to gain the judges confidence. He approaches the judge, takes a deep breath.

"My case file is clear as day. You need not waste your precious time reading his made up dossier. All you need to do is ask Haj Agha Salehi."

The judge suddenly looks up at the mention of this name and begins to listen to Sassan with interest. Sassan seems reassured after seeing the judges reaction.

"Haj Agha, in those days,"

He points to Arash.

"long ago, when I was only 13-14 years old, when this little shit was safely tucked away here in England, I was fighting Saddam Hussein's invading army at the front line."

The judge listens closely, Sassan seems content to have gained the judges attention. Sassan looks at Arash mockingly.

THE IRAN-IRAQ FRONTLINE

The thunder of howitzers and exploding shells can be heard in the distance. A group of about fifteen 13-14 year olds wearing military uniforms, boots and green bandannas take cover behind a hill. Sassan who is fourteen years old is the group's leader and is drilling the rest. The young men are standing in a line and taking turns running and jumping over a stick being held about a metre above the ground by two boys. The sun is beginning to set. Explosions could still be heard. An older soldier appears from behind the hill and walks towards them.

THE SOLDIER: *Calls loudly*

"Sassan Yazdani!"

Sassan quickly goes to him and gives him a military salute.

THE SOLDIER: *"Haj Agha Salehi wants you to get your group organised and ready, he is going to send you on a mission. Get ready and follow me."*

SASSAN: *Says forcefully*

"Yes Sergeant"

He turns to the other boys

"We have been summoned. Everyone follow me."

They all begin to follow the soldiers, in a short distance, Haj Agha Salehi who is a 45 year old bearded cleric wearing a black robe and turban gets out of a jeep. He is surrounded by several revolutionary guards.

SASSAN: *He stops near Haj Agha Salehi and turns to the group*

"Attention!"

All the young boys organize themselves into a line and stand to attention. Sassan stands in front. The other soldiers also form a line behind Haj Agha Salehi. The cleric stands between the soldiers and Sassan's group. A few shells cause panic as they explode nearby. They all turn and look toward the area where the shells fell. Smoke and dust rise into the air.

SALEHI: *He points to a soldier who is holding a box. The box contains a bunch of plastic keys. A chain is attached to each key. Sassan goes to Haj Agha Salehi as he signals him over.*

"Have your men step forward one at a time so that I can hang a key to heaven around their necks."

Sassan begins to call his men by their names. They each approach Haj Agha Salehi , take a short bow and then lower their heads. Haj Agha Salehi hangs a key around their necks. They go back and stand in line. Haj Agha Salehi paces back and forth in front of them. Except for distant explosions, no other sound can be heard.

SALEHI: *"Dear sons of Islam! I have some very good and uplifting news for you this evening. Last night, a Seyyed whose ancestry goes back all the way to the great Imam (Saint) Hussein and whom I greatly respect, told me that he had a dream that the great Mahdi (the Messiah) will appear riding his white horse near sunset today."*

They all say loudly "praise be upon him, may god bless all the descendants of the holy prophet Mohammad"

"My blessed sons of Islam, you must break through this minefield this evening and reach the great Imam on the other side." There is a small commotion amongst the group. "Should you, who are indeed the pride and soul of Islam be able to obtain the elevated place of martyrdom, which is the hope and dream of each and everyone of us," He begins to sob.

"you shall rise to the heavens at his holiness's side and walk straight into heaven. If you are not martyred, the least this mission will bring you is for you to gaze upon his holiness's heavenly face and this is an exceptional opportunity."

They all follow Haj Agha Salehi as he signals them to follow him. They stop as they reach the top of a small hill. The sound of distant explosions can still be heard. Haj Agha Salehi begins to speak with one of the officers. The young boys are all standing in line facing the front. One of the officers orders a soldier to erect two black flags on either side of the line. Everyone is nervously waiting. It is slowly getting dark. Some of the boys point to something in the distance.

SASSAN: *He cries loudly "Holy Imam Mahdi!"*

All the boys repeat loudly "Holy Imam Mahdi"

SALEHI: *"My children, his holiness has arrived. Hurry."*

The boys rush toward a rider in the distance wearing all white and riding a white horse. As they run through the minefield several of the boys are thrown into the air as some of the mines explode. It is almost completely dark. Only a few of the boys are left still standing. The voice of one of the boys can be heard through the dust covered minefield. The boy is calling Sassan's name. He sees Sassan through the haze caused by the explosion's and walks towards him while sobbing aloud.

THE BOY: *"Sassan, the Iraqi's just martyred the Imam and his horse."*

He points.

SASSAN: *"Are you sure?"*

The boy nods as he continues to whimper

"We must quickly take this news to Haj Agha Salehi. Hurry we must get back quickly."

They both begin to run. Explosions can still be heard from near and far. The boy is running close to Sassan. Suddenly another mine explosion is heard. Sassan turns and sees his friend rolling on the ground all covered in blood and in pain. He goes towards him. He soon realizes that his friend has been killed. He has also been wounded. His foot is bleeding, his hand is bloodied. He starts to run again. He is limping. He gets to the other side of the field. He quickly gets to Haj Agha Salehi who is surrounded by some soldiers and officers.

SASSAN: *While breathing heavily*

"Haj Agha, Haj Agha"

Sassan begins to cry as Haj Agha Salehi approaches him.

"The Iraqi's just martyred the great Imam and his horse. All of the members of the group have also been martyred."

Sassan collapses onto the ground.

SALEHI*: Turns to the soldiers.*

"Quickly get this lad to the field hospital. He has been badly wounded. He looks like he has lost a lot of blood."

The soldiers quickly lift Sassan up and hurry away.

THE FIELD HOSPITAL

In a large tent, a few wounded soldiers lie on their beds moaning and groaning in pain. Sassan is lying on one of the beds. His foot is bandaged, he is covered with a white sheet. He is awake and staring at the ceiling. Haj Agha Salehi enters the tent accompanied by a few men. Sassan tries to sit up on the bed when he sees him.

SALEHI: *Looks at Sassan*

"No, don't sit up, your stitches will come apart and you will start to bleed again. Just relax my son."

Sassan kisses the Haj Agha's hand and lies back down. A chair is fetched for the Haj Agha and placed next to Sassan's bed. He sits on the chair next to Sassan and feels his forehead.

"Thank god your fever has gone down. You must rest. By the way I wanted to let you know that the person the Iraqi's killed was one of the local villagers going home on his donkey. My son you must remember that no earthly human can ever bring any harm to his holiness the great Imam Mahdi. Today you will be honoured with the title 'Walking Martyre'."

"It was by the grace of the great Imam that you are alive and among us. You performed your mission exemplarily. The path that you and your group cleared through the minefield allowed the soldiers to be able to reach the enemy infidels and destroy them. You are being sent home tomorrow. You don't have to be at the front any longer. May the dear Lord watch over you."

THE COURTROOM

SASSAN AND NAZANINE'S TRIAL

Sassan appears to be searching for something in his pocket. The judge and Arash are both looking at him with curiosity.

SASSAN: *"Haj Agha please allow me to show you my commendation letter that I was presented for my bravery and acts of courage at the war front. Haj Agha Salehi personally handed this to me. The elevated title of 'Walking Martyre' is written on the top alongside his signature."*

Sassan is looking into all of his pockets, he is trying hard to find the letter. He takes his jacket off and begins to look into the pockets, but is unable to find it. Arash smiles. The judge also laughs at Sassan. Arash gets up and whispers something into the judges ear. Haj Agha and Arash both point to a page. Haj Agha looks at Sassan with disdain. Sassan goes quiet and sits down.

SASSAN: *In an angry tone*

"Do you judges expect us to carry a ton of documents with us everywhere we go!"

Arash laughs at him and points out another page in the file to Haj Agha.

"Haj Agha, I swear to god this weasel is lying to you. Please don't believe a word he says."

The judge who has now gone through every page in the file closes it and looks at Sassan. At his signal, Arash comes to Haj Agha and sits next to him. Sassan faces them feeling like a condemned man who has now nothing else to fear.

"O.K., go ahead and believe what your dear Arash has to say. So what? Now what are you going to do to us? You are the one who killed the

Colonel, his two sons and his brother. You sent his wife to the grave with anguish and sorrow. Haven't you done enough? You confiscated everything they owned."

He screams.

"You blood sucking leach. What more do you want from us?"

He walks toward the judge and Arash and looks at both of them with great loathing and disdain.

"You are both the same. Paid agents, British lackys."

The loud sound of the gavel brought down by the English judge brings Sassan out of his stupor. He pulls himself together and sits up in the chair. Everyone stands. The judge exits the court. Sassan looks weak and pale. He seems to have lost all hope. Nazanine while still whimpering approaches him along with Arash. Sassan puts his hand around her waist consolingly. Nazanine puts her head on Sassan's shoulder. The solicitors are discussing something amongst each other.

ARASH: *He approaches Sassan and Nazanine*

"Unfortunately, the court session has taken much longer than usual today Mrs. Afshar, the judge has postponed your trial until tomorrow. The court will resume tomorrow morning at 9:00am sharp. You can leave now, but make sure to be here before 9:00am tomorrow morning."

"Would you like me to walk to the bus stop with you to make sure you get on the right bus and not end up on the other side of London?"

SASSAN: *Angrily*

"No thanks, we know what bus to get on."

In a sarcastic and disdainful tone

"It is not at all necessary. Don't bother. We shall find the way."

Sassan and Nazanine begin to walk toward the exit and leave. Arash follows them with his eyes as they approach the exit. Arash shakes his head and takes a deep breath.

SASSAN: *Sassan and Nazanine are walking toward the bus stop along the pavement.*

"The idiot thinks we just escaped from the jungles of Africa and haven't seen a bus before."

Thinks for a bit.

"Maybe he wants to extract some more information from us again and tell the Home Office solicitor? I am willing to swear that this fellow has never helped a single soul in his life. Now all of a sudden how come he suddenly feels concerned that we might not be able to find our bus? Yes sure he is going to come with us and help us. Help us my foot. He isn't getting away with it this time."

NAZANINE: "How did I do during questioning?"

Sassan stays silent.

"Were the answers I gave alright? Were they O.K.? What do you think? Is there possibly any hope?"

SASSAN: *Sighs* "I don't really know. It all depends on the way this weasel translated what you said."

NAZANINE: *They have arrived at the bus stop*

"Well, I told them everything I knew. I got everything off my chest. Whatever will be will be."

In the meantime a double-decker bus pulls into the bus stop. They both get on.

ARASH AND SARAH'S HOUSE

5:30PM

Sarah has made herself up and is wearing a colourful dress. She leaves the kitchen carrying a bowl of salad. She places the salad bowl on the dining table and goes to the kitchen again. She returns carrying three plates, spoons and forks. Soft music fills the room. The weather is nice and warm. The sun is shining. The door to the sitting room is open. The sun rays fill the room. The door bell rings. Sarah opens the door. Arash comes in. Sarah and Arash kiss each other.

SARAH: *As they enter the sitting room*

"You are right on time dear. I was just setting the dinner table."

She looks at Arash.

"You look very tired dear!?"

ARASH: *"The court went into session very late."*

Arash sits on the couch, he places his briefcase on the floor next to him. He takes a large box out of a plastic bag.

SARAH: *"How was the court today?"*

Kian's footsteps can be heard coming down the stairs.

ARASH: *"Same as usual.....I will tell you after dinner."*

KIAN: *Walks in*

"Hello dad."

He sits on the couch next to Arash. Sarah returns to the kitchen.

KIAN: *Excitedly*

"Oh, wow, a sony laptop. Thank you so much. It is exactly what I wanted."

Kian kisses Arashes face. He takes the box from him and runs upstairs.

SARAH*: In a loud voice*

"Dinner will be ready in five minutes."

ARASH*: As he climbs the stairs*

"Place that bottle of vodka in the freezer so that it is nice and cold. I feel like having a couple of shots together after dinner."

SARAH*: "Sure, that's not a bad idea. Specially this evening with this great weather we are having. I don't mind having a little either."*

IN THE GARDEN AT ARASH'S HOUSE

THE SUN IS BEGINNING TO SET

There is a small garden at the back of the house, some bushes and shrubs are planted along the wooden fence on both sides. Rose bushes and other flowers thrive in the garden. The sitting room door that opens into the garden is ajar, a few garden chairs can be seen around a table placed on the stone covered patio area. Arash is wearing a brown jumper and is sitting on a chair facing the garden. A bottle of vodka, a bottle of lemonade and a bowl of crisps and nuts can be seen on the table in front of him. Sarah is sitting across from him wearing comfortable clothes. They are both holding a glass.

SARAH: *Turns to Arash as she takes a sip of vodka.*

"I drink to you and the children's health."

ARASH: *Raises his glass*

"To you and the kids. You are all I have in this world."

SARAH: *"I have some very good news for you."*

As she smiles at Arash

"Guess what it is. Close your eyes, I want to show you something."

Arash smiles and nods in agreement. Sarah quickly enters the sitting room. After a brief moment she peeks out of the sitting room door.

SARAH: *"Ready? Then close your eyes."*

Arash closes his eyes. Sarah enters the garden holding a glass frame and a large envelope. She hands a nicely framed commendation letter to Arash.

SARAH: *"Don't open your eyes yet."*

She quickly takes out a tissue out of the box and wipes the frame.

"O.K., now you can open your eyes."

Arash does not seem that excited, he just looks at the frame and smiles.

"Bravo, well done. With this commendation letter you have brought honour to the family. Look at what prominent people have signed the bottom of this letter."

Sarah kisses Arash on the cheeks.

"I haven't told the children yet. I thought I should tell you before I let the children know. I couldn't wait and told my brother and parents though. All the relatives probably know by now. We are going to throw a party this weekend when all the children and their friends come home. We will kill two birds with one stone. You can't imagine how happy mother was. She was so overjoyed that she started to cry. You don't know how much they love you. They believe that one kinder, truer and nicer than you hasn't been born. They broke the mould when they made you."

Arash looks at Sarah.

ARASH: *"What do you think of me?"*

SARAH: *with slight amazement*

"Surely you know that I love you from the bottom of my heart."

"You are a kind, compassionate and loyal husband to me and a giving and selfless father to the children."

She sighs

"God forbid if one of the kids falls ill, I have seen the way you give up food and sleep and take care of them until they get well. The children too love you from the bottom of their hearts and respect you. That is what I think about you."

ARASH: *Takes a deep breath and finishes his drink*

"I wish at least one tenth of these refugees would think well of me."

SARAH: *Changes the subject. She picks the large envelope up off the* *table and holds it in front of Arash.*

"You didn't ask me what this is?"

ARASH: *As he pours himself some vodka*

"O.K., what's in the envelope?"

SARAH: *Takes a magazine and a letter out of the envelope and happily shows them to Arash.*

"After thanking you for your work, they are asking that you hold a class once a week and lecture to the newly hired Home Office interpreters. Be like a university professor, teach them how to become a great, professional and true translator like yourself. What is interesting is that these are not just farsi translators, you can find translators from every corner of the world amongst them. Well this is a great development in your career. I did a little figuring, your salary will almost double. This is great."

She raises her glass and faces Arash.

"To a great future for us all."

He also raises his glass and takes a gulp.

"By the way, I made a few copies of this commendation letter so that you can carry a few in your briefcase, incase you wish to give a copy to your friends."

ARASH: *"Thank you my dear."*

The magazine captures his eye.

"What is that?"

SARAH: *Hands a small booklet that is not more than about 20 pages thick to Arash.*

"This was inside the envelope. It is about the class and the convention that is to be held for the new interpreters. They want you to teach them to become professionals so that they won't waste the courts time."

ARASH: *Tries to change the subject*

"Did Kian like his laptop?"

SARAH: *"Yes, very much so. He is downloading some programmes and CD's onto it. He is very excited."*

She turns to Arash who is staring at the garden.

"Are you alright? Recently you seem a bit tired and restless. Anything the matter?"

She pauses for a moment

"How was court today?"

ARASH: *Pours some vodka for her and himself, drops a few pieces of ice in the glass and pours some lemonade over them.*

"I was translating for a refugee couple called Sassan and Nazanine. The court began very late and couldn't be concluded today. They will resume tomorrow morning."

SARAH: *Sympathetically "I know what you are saying. It gets to be a bore. These few hours in a courtroom without getting anywhere could be quite tiring."*

ARASH: *"No not at all. It's really not that tiring to me. I usually read a book or my paper. Write something. I somehow amuse myself. I am used to these delays."*

SARAH: *"What's the matter then? Why are you so down? Something is bothering you isn't it?"*

ARASH: *"Today I felt for a while that this couple had me on trial."*

SARAH: *Sips her drink "What do you mean?"*

ARASH: *"Sometimes I feel that I am torn between two very different cultures, a clash of civilizations."*

He pauses for a moment before he says...

"You know very well Sarah, for many years I have been interpreting loyally and honestly for this court system. I have been true to both my job and when it came to upholding the law. Whatever the judge and the solicitors said I translated verbatim."

SARAH: *Looks amazed*

"Well surely you haven't done anything wrong have you? What else were you supposed to do? You did what was expected of you."

ARASH: *"Yes, you are right, You see these people are my fellow compatriots or at least farsi speakers. They are strangers here, mostly desperate. They consider me to be one of them. They expect me to help them. But this is against the law and my creed. It doesn't work that way."*

SARAH: *"Well their expectations are unjustified. What can you do for them?"*

ARASH: *"Not much, but still that doesn't mean that they won't expect things."*

He looks at Sarah and says...

"Do you remember about 7-8 years ago when I represented an Iranian Kurd who along with a young boy had survived a trip across in a container in which three Chinese refugees lost their lives?"

SARAH: *As she nods her head*

"Oh yes, yes I remember it well. His name was Rafat. The one that was later executed by the regime taking part in an armed struggle against the Islamic Republic."

ARASH: *"Bravo. What an amazing memory. Today, when we were waiting I told Sassan and Nazanine about Rafat's ordeal. They were both quite affected and upset, especially Nazanine. She asked if I felt a lot of guilt and remorse for not being able to help that young Kurd. When I said that I didn't, they were very surprised.*

SARAH: *"You shouldn't take her too seriously. Forget it. These ignorant refugees are not familiar with the laws of this country."*

ARASH: *"Sometimes it's very hard to ignore some of the things these people say."*

He takes a deep breath.

"Despite the fact that many years have passed since that incident, I don't know but for some reason once Nazanine asked that question, I suddenly felt very sorry for Rafat. I don't know why I was so saddened? He was

so young and so well mannered. He asked the judge to forgive him for having entered England illegally."

SARAH: *"If you remember, I was very upset too. This is natural, but why should you feel guilty? Even now when you mention it, I feel so sorry and sad for that young man."*

ARASH: *Drinks a little vodka*

"You are my wife and my soul mate. I can never tell you a lie. The truth is that today after the conversation I had with this couple, I felt guilty for the first time during my career translating. I asked myself why I had never stepped over the line to save the life of at least one of these miserable souls. I could have at least not translated if they said something contradictory that would hurt their case? Sometimes I wonder why I haven't crossed the red line of my moral and legal duty and translated something different in order to help their case."

"Believe me, I have come to know what this Home Office solicitor is going to say before he even opens his mouth. I know what he is going to ask and the hidden purpose behind his questions. I have never committed a wrong while translating. I related whatever I heard to the court word for word regardless, whether what they said hurt or helped their case."

SARAH: *In approval*

"I completely believe you. That is obvious."

She points to the commendation letter.

"If it was any different, they would not have honoured you with this. Such an honour, signed by so many dignitaries, judges, barristers, men of significance."

ARASH: *"With what Sassan and Nazanine brought up and the questions they kept asking me, I felt like I was being tried before my own conscience."*

SARAH: *"When do you think their trial is over? Do you think they have any chance of being granted a visa?"*

ARASH: *"I think it should be over by noon tomorrow. Today, Nazanine was the only one questioned. The poor thing cried so much. Her tears* seemed genuine. She is absolutely terrified of their appeal being rejected and being sent back to Iran."

Sarah turns the lights on. It is beginning to get dark. Arash takes a sip of his drink.

"I don't think that the judge will rule in their favour at all. They couldn't provide a single document to back up their claims and the judge, Peter Jones, and the Home Office barrister don't give sobs and tears much weight. They require witnesses and hard evidence which this couple lack."

SARAH: "Are you sure that they weren't acting? I mean could this be made-up? Same as many of the others?"

ARASH: As he shakes his head in disagreement.

"No, no, I don't think so."

He hesitates before saying...

"But there was a story Nazanine told regarding how her father the Colonel and her uncle were badly beaten, tortured and then taken away and executed by the revolutionary guard. I am pretty sure that I heard a very similar story somewhere before, but I couldn't quite put my finger on it."

SARAH: "I presume that one of these many asylum seekers related a similar story to the court before?"

ARASH: "Probably. I guess that is possible."

SARAH: Looks at her watch

"At what time do you have to be in court tomorrow?"

ARASH: "9:00am sharp."

SARAH: "It's 10:15 now. You better get some sleep. You had a tiring day as usual. I will clear the table, take care of dishes quickly and join you upstairs."

ARASH: He gets off the chair

"Let me help you dear. We will clear the table together."

SARAH: *"Thanks love, but you are so tired, leave it to me and go to bed. I'll join you in a few minutes.*

ARASH: *"Very well."*

Arash climbs the stairs and enters the bedroom.

ARASH AND SARAH'S HOUSE

BEDROOM

Arash and Sarah are both wearing white bed clothes and asleep. A pale light covers the room. Arash is deep asleep. He seems to be dreaming. One could hear him speak in his sleep.

ARASH: *Speaks in a clear and understandable tone*

"Jeff, oh Jeff, why have you brought me here?"

HYDE PARK

SPEAKER'S CORNER

The speakers corner is a gathering place located within London's Hyde Park where anyone could come and freely express his or her opinions and beliefs. This place is one of the symbols of British free society.

Arash dreams that he is entering Hyde Park accompanied by Jeff. It is around midnight. The light that can be seen comes from the tall lamp-posts around the park. The park is almost dark. Jeff, who is wearing a dark suit, white shirt and a blue tie is carrying several folders under his arm. Arash wearing a brown suit, white shirt and brightly coloured tie is carrying a samsonite briefcase. They are walking along a dimly lit path.

ARASH: *"Why have you brought me here at this time of night? I thought the trial for the immigrants was being held at the court house not Hyde Park?"*

JEFF: *"Mr Peter Jones, the presiding judge, ordered it."*

He continues after a moment

"As you know we must follow his directions. This is the gathering point. Everyone will be here soon."

ARASH: *"I don't have any idea what you are talking about? If there is a trial to be held, it should be at the court house, not at Hyde Park and the speakers corner at that?!"*

JEFF: *Points to a large crowd that is approaching from a distance. "Mr. Arash Vaziri, would it be possible to fit this large crowd inside a courtroom? You judge for yourself, would it? Of course not."*

ARASH: *Points to the large torch carrying crowd that is approaching them* as they sing an anthem. *"Now, why are they carrying all those blazing torches? God forbid I hope they don't put the trees in the park on fire. With this insolent noise at this time of the night they are going to wake people up."*

JEFF: *Faces Arash as he looks at one of the pages in the file he is holding. "As far as I know these torches are supposed to represent the fire of hatred and loathing that burn in their heart. This is a symbolic act. They have asked permission from the court to carry these."*

ARASH: *"That is very interesting, I had never seen or heard of such a thing. Believe me Jeff, I am serious."*

JEFF: *"Well now you can see it with your own eyes. Of course this is going to be an interesting experience for me too."*

The sound of singing can now be heard from the distance.

"From injustice and oppression we flee

through the air, land or the sea.

Beloved home and country never to see.

The devil has the people by the throat.

As we wander into strange lands so remote

with mere hopes and dreams,

the borders we cross

threading in much peril as in god we entrust.

Our future, our dreams.

But all to nothing it sadly seems.

Into dust it all turned, into ashes it all burned.

Alas Alas Alas. It was all mirages, mirages and mirages.

We are all guilty as charged.

We are exile refugees. Plaintiffs looking for justice."

ARASH: *"Are these all asylum seekers? Wow. That is a nice anthem they are singing. They sound like soldiers returning from battle."*

JEFF: *"Actually quite the opposite. They sound like soldiers on their way to battle!" Opens a folder and shows it to Arash*

"No these people are not asking for asylum. They are all plaintiffs. Of course they had asked for asylum at one time but were denied. Now they are complaining."

ARASH: *"Oh, I thought they are all asylum seekers.*

After a deep breath.

"By the way what are these people complaining about?"

The people chant

"From injustice and oppression we flee

through the air, land or the sea.

Beloved home and country never to see.

The devil has the people by the throat.

As we wander into strange lands so remote

with mere hopes and dreams,

the borders we cross

threading in much peril as in god we entrust.

Our future, our dreams.

But all to nothing it sadly seems.

Into dust it all turned, into ashes it all burned.

alas alas alas. It was all mirages, mirages and mirages.

We are all guilty as charged.

We are exile refugees. Plaintiffs looking for justice."

"To whom can one complain?"

JEFF: *Refers to the case file again. "These people have all filed complaints against you Mr. Vaziri."*

ARASH: *He seems shocked. After a few moments he begins to laugh out loud.*

"You are pulling my leg aren't you? You have brought me here to Hyde Park in the middle of the night to play some kind of a joke on me haven't you? Very funny." He laughs again.

JEFF: "Don't you at all remember them? Look carefully."

Hands a file to Arash.

ARASH: "Oh yes" He laughs as he looks at Jeff. "We are having a surprise party?! Is the band on it's way? With the anthems these people are singing, might as well have had a few musicians along to bring some life to the party. Maybe a few belly dancers too."

He begins to laugh again.

"Then we can all complain against one another. Look at these people."

The crowd has formed a 20 metre wide circle around them.

JEFF: *Shouts at Arash.*

"What the hell are you talking about Mr. Vaziri? All their names are on this list. Take your time and have a bloody look and see if you remember. They are all plaintiffs."

Arash goes quiet and looks at the list.

"You were their court translator. Aren't I right?"

ARASH: Looks at the list "Yes, that is correct. This is a list of all the people whom I translated for. So what are they saying? What the hell do they want from me?"

JEFF: "They are claiming that you did not properly translate what they

had to say in the courtroom which resulted in them being denied visas and being given permission to stay in this country. That's their complaint."

ARASH: Pleading "For god sake, tell them to go away. I don't feel like dealing with them now."

JEFF: "Do you know what you are talking about? These poor souls have travelled thousands of miles to speakers corner to be able to speak their minds.

ARASH: Angrily

"I hope they all choke on their words. Tell them to go back to wherever they came from."

JEFF: *Angrily*

"Have you got no shame? Now you have become a dictator too?"

While screaming

"This is the speakers corner. In this place anyone can say anything they wish. People can even criticize the Prime Minister or the Queen if they wished without harbouring any fear. Now, how dare you say that they shouldn't criticize you? Do you think that you are above the Queen of England? Apparently, you don't believe in the freedom of speech. You fear criticism. Why shouldn't these poor souls be able to speak at this sacred location that symbolizes freedom of speech in the whole world?"

ARASH: *"Then inform Mr Peter Jones to come here and be the judge. I am not prepared, for one moment to listen to these stupid accusations."*

JEFF: *"Mr. Vaziri, you seem to be ignoring what I am telling you. It is actually Mr Peter Jones's order that you must meet with these people. You were the one who translated their words to the court. Not Mr. Jones. Secondly, if you translated what they had to say properly and correctly, what then do you have to fear? You should at least listen to what they have to say."*

ARASH: *Points to the people approaching them*

"Jeff, tell these people to back off for a minute. I want to talk to you about something first in private."

Jeff signals to the torch carrying crowd with his hand.

The crowd stops.

ARASH: *Looks at the crowd each carrying a torch and gathered in a circle around them.*

"I am sure you follow, like everyone else, the news regarding parliamentary elections. You do realise that what will probably decide these elections is the policies these party's will adopt toward immigration issues and the flood of refugees into this country. This is the most sensitive issue of the

day. It is the wish of most of the people in this country to stop the flood of illegal immigrants. You very well know that tens of thousands of illegals are freely walking about as we speak. Secondly, Mr. Jeff Wilkinson, you have known me for many years and you know that I have great regard for you. Let me ask you, have you ever known me to have faultered in my work? As god is my witness I only followed the court's rules and regulations. I translated whatever these people said verbatim. The same applies to whatever the solicitors and the judge had to say."

He leans towards Jeff.

"You can't imagine the things these people expected of me? I had never said this to anyone. But I guess I will have to tell you."

Jeff seems indifferent.

"They all expected me to translate what they said in a manner that would be pleasing to the judges palate, against the commitments that I had made."

"They would ask me not to translate anything that might hurt their case. Or to twist their words in such a way that would help them win their case and so that they will all be given visas and granted permanent stay. They expected me to break the law to ignore the commitments I have made to this establishment. Please hand that file to me for a minute."

Jeff hands Arash the file.

"I want to point out some of these names to you."

He opens the file and shows it to Jeff. Jeff leans towards the file and looks at the page that Arash is indicating.

"This fellow, Mohsen Abbasi and this one and also this one, they all asked me to put in a good word for them with the judge. Also to make up a suitable answer whenever the judge or the Home Office solicitor asked a question, without paying any attention to the answers which they gave. Dear Mr. Wilkinson, please pay good attention to this issue. They had thought that since the judge and the solicitor did not speak any farsi, I could just make up anything I wished as we went along, that meant for me to cross the red line. To forget my work ethics. To become a law breaker like them. This Mr. Mohsen Abbasi that is carrying a blazing torch and screaming like a hooligan

tried to bribe me with a silk carpet woven in Kashan, some pistachio nuts from Kerman and a few miniature paintings made in Esfahan. He sent them to my house along with a message that I should divide these between the judge, myself and the Home Office solicitor."

"He thought that like Iran, one can get things done through bribe and favouritism. I returned all these goods to him along with a few unmentionable words."

JEFF: Quickly turns the file's pages

"Yes, but Mr. Abbasi claimed that this was a gift for you from his family in Iran and that you had taken it all wrong. He said these were mere souvenirs that he had brought for you from Iran. This is a private family issue and does not concern the court at all. Especially when the person concerned confessed to it himself."

ARASH: While smiling

"My dear friend. This guy Abbasi is lying through his teeth. There isn't a straight bone in his body. You should study this fellow's file. We didn't hear this fellow utter one straight word on the day of his trial. He spoke in contradictions. He had everyone confused. Just look at how Peter Jones ruled on this case. This Abbasi was screaming and yelling half the time. He dropped his pants right in front of the judge and everyone else in the room. He wasn't a bit ashamed. At the end the judge angrily had him removed from the courtroom."

JEFF: Closes the file

"What you just said and the court documents will have nothing to do with what has been planned for tonight. However, I will speak with Mr. Abbasi and see what he has to say."

ARASH: "No my dear Mr. Wilkinson. There is no need for that. You do not need to say anything to him about this. Just get rid of these people. It is 1:30am for pete's sake. You too are tired. We must both attend court tomorrow morning."

JEFF: Angrily

"Mr Vaziri! This is the speakers corner. People come here from all over the world to speak their minds without fear. Not only are you thinking about stopping these people from saying what is on their minds, but you are also trying to shut me up too. The people who are gathered here tonight are all here to complain about you. They want to be able to speak in a free atmosphere. You have no choice but to listen to what they have to say."

ARASH: *"In that case, I have a complaint about everyone of these people. They all encouraged me to break the law, but I never gave in. I am proud of that."*

JEFF: *Speaks calmly*

"O.K. fine. You can climb on top of that three legged stool after they are done and speak your heart out. No-one is stopping you. There is democracy in this country. Especially here at Hyde Park's speakers corner. Everyone here can say whatever they want to say."

With a hand gesture from Jeff, the crowd approaches them. They form two concentric circles at 8 and 5 metres from Jeff respectively. Arash is frightened. He is staring at the blazing torches being waived by the crowd. He suddenly recognizes Saeed within one of the circles. He points to Saeed who is wearing a skirt and a blouse and carrying a ladies handbag. Saeed's face looks all bloodied.

ARASH: *"Is this Saeed that same asylum seeker who had claimed to be gay?"*

As he faces Jeff

"Why is his face all bloody? Was he in an accident?"

JEFF: *Turns to the file*

"Yes, this gentleman.....well lady, is Saeed for whom you translated and the judge ordered to be deported. He was beaten almost to death by the militants near the city theatre in Daneshjoo Park. He blames all his misfortunes on you and is also really furious with you. Look at his torch, the blazing flames that you see are a symbol of the fire that is burning in his heart. The hatred that he harbours for you."

ARASH: *Is scared, he looks around. "Why have they surrounded us in* *this way?"*

JEFF: *Leans forward* *"They want to make sure that you don't have some plot brewing in your pretty head to escape. That's why they have formed a circle around us." He looks at Arash.*

"Do you see the blazing flames of their anger and loathing? You had better stop even thinking about escape tonight, since you don't have a bloody chance!"

ARASH: *Pleading "For heaven's sake, please help me get away from this situation. Have mercy on your old chum. Find a way out."*

JEFF: *Takes a deep breath*

"I can't think of any way out of this. Please be ready to listen to what each one of these people has to say."

ARASH: *As if he has had an idea immediately opens his briefcase and takes out a copy of his commendation letter and hands it to Jeff.*

"I was presented this by the court for many years of loyal and honest service and being true to the laws and rules of translating."

He points at the bottom of the page to Jeff

"Look, every judge and Home Office lawyer has signed this."

"This document proves that I have never taken a wrong step while performing my duties and unlike some of the immigration judges I have never allowed my emotions to get the best of me."

Turns to Jeff.

"They have asked me to form a class for the new translators and to teach them as to how to perform their work professionally and honestly as I do."

JEFF: *He looks at the pages of the commendation letter.*

"Well, what do you want me to do with these?"

ARASH: *"Isn't it obvious? I want you to hand each of them a copy. Then tell them that Mr. Arash Vaziri is recognized by all the immigration judges and Home Office solicitors."*

Jeff looks at the copies.

ARASH CONTINUES*: "Show them all these signatures. There are more than 20 names here. That should surely be enough."*

JEFF*: "Are you sure you know what you are talking about? Have you thought about this?"*

ARASH*: Desperately*

"Yes. This is the only document that I have with me tonight. Don't give more than one copy to each person so that they can all have one. I wrote the Farsi translation on the back so that they can all read it. What are you waiting for?"

Jeff hesitates.

"Once they read this they will hopefully go away and leave us alone. What are you waiting for then? Go on. Make sure this Mr. Abbasi gets a copy. This might help diminish the blazing flames of his hatred. He is a dangerous and violent man. I don't trust this person at all."

Jeff goes towards the crowd and begins to hand each one a copy of the letter. He walks through the first circle and hands a few copies to the crowd standing around in the outer ring. A commotion erupts within the crowd. The crowd are screaming loudly and Jeff is trying to calm them down.

Some begin to burn the copies that they have been handed. The crowd becomes louder and more aroused.

THE CROWD*: begin to chant in unison*

"Arash Vaziri is our sworn enemy. We express our anger through the blazing flames of the torches that you see."

Jeff tries to quiet down the crowd. Everyone goes silent. The crowd standing in the first ring around Arash lower their torches together and point them toward Arash. Jeff quickly approaches Arash.

JEFF*: "With this stupid commendation letter you added fuel to this crowds fire. Look at how these torches have gone ablaze and the heat with which they are burning. If I hadn't managed to calm them down they would have* burnt you at the stake using these same torches. I think you better see to Robabeh and her young martyred son first. The old woman has come a very long way and hasn't any strength left. Shall I call her? Are you ready?"

ARASH: *While pleading*

"Can't I see the old woman tomorrow night? I am not at all up to it at the moment. I have a nasty headache. My knees are shaking with exhaustion. I think I have the flu. I have a fever."

He starts to cry.

"No... No... I can't face this old biddy, I am ill don't you understand!"

Cries desperately

"Please … please …I beg you Jeff"

JEFF: *Angry and frustrated points at Arash and in a loud voice shouts*

"Stop it! For God's sake you are sobbing and crying like a little spoilt boy, be a man and don't shy away from this old and fragile woman"

Jeff pauses for a short while and after a deep breath he tries with a calm voice to convince Arash

"Don't you get it? This poor and destitute woman just wants to get something off her chest and go and get on with her life. She can't see very well. She has brought Rafat along to be her guide.

ARASH: *As if he has no choice.*

"It seems as if I have no alternative but to meet and speak with them. But Jeff, please don't go anywhere, for petes sake stay and control this crowd. I am really horrified."

JEFF: "O.K. I agree."

"How about if we pull that wooden bench over so that Rafat and his mother can stand on it and get whatever complaints or problems they have with you off their chests once and for all. God willing their anger and hatred might subside."

With a signal from Jeff, two men in the crowd grab the bench and place it on the ground not far from Arash and Jeff. Robabeh gets on the bench with Rafat's help. Rafat looks pale and ghostly. A hangman's noose is around his neck and the end of the rope is hanging down to his knees. He gets on the bench and holds his mother's hand.

ROBABEH: *Turns to Rafat "Point out Arash the interpreter to me."*

Rafat points to Arash. Jeff softly nudges Arash forward who is almost hiding himself behind him.

ROBABEH: *"Mr. Arash, you had my young son unfairly executed. You practically put the noose around his neck with the rubbish that you said in court." As she cries in anger.*

"I will never get over my son's death. I will never forgive you."

Turns to Jeff.

"I cried so much that my eyes can't see well anymore. This man Arash broke my heart, he took a piece of my heart and soul from me. I will mourn my son Rafat until the day I die."

She continues to weep.

"I now have no one left in this world to take care of me."

ARASH: *In a loud voice*

"Dear madam, I swear to god, I am not to blame. It was Mr. Peter Jones the judge who ordered him deported."

"It's not my fault."

Jeff asks Arash to be quiet.

ROBABEH: *"My poor young son had to spend 14 hungry and thirsty days inside a hot and cramped metal box. With a thousand trials and tribulations and a heart full of hope he managed to escape the claws of death and reach this country. Mr. Vaziri, not only did you not help him, you actually caused the judge to decide to deport him with your wrong and unfair translations. I have no complaints about the judge. It is you whom I am complaining about. You, you heartless louse, you bloodsucking murderer!"*

ARASH: *"Dear madam, none of what they have told you is true. I translated whatever your son said, word for word. This is my legal duty. You must consider this. I am a servant of the court and not your son's solicitor."*

ROBABEH: *"You cruel and heartless man. You son of a bitch. You sent* *my son to his death."*

She faces the crowd who are all chanting in her support.

"This shameless coward told the judge that my son did not speak with a Kurdish accent. Talk you bastard. Isn't it so? Can you even tell us what a Kurdish accent sounds like? How was he supposed to speak? When you yourself told the judge that you couldn't speak Kurdish, then how could you tell whether he spoke with a Kurdish accent or not? Huh? Talk....."

Goes quiet.

"With this one word of untruth that you told the judge, you literally issued the deportation orders, a death sentence for my poor Rafat, my flesh and blood."

The crowd cry in unison.

"Arash Vaziri is our sworn enemy. We express our anger through the torches you see."

Robabeh and Rafat get off the benches and join the crowd.

ARASH: *Worriedly turns to Jeff*

"Please allow me to say my piece then. I must defend myself. To be fair it is now my turn to address the crowd and clear things up and get it over with. I worked with honesty and sincerity all of my life and now a conspiracy has been organised against me. They have accused me of being a murderer. A killer. This is far from fair. I must speak and answer these accusations."

JEFF: *Looks at the crowd*

"They have all taken turns to speak way before you. First you must wait until all these people have stood on the bench and said their piece."

Turns to Arash.

"You know very well that all these people have a lot bottled up inside them against you."

ARASH: *"It will take three to four nights before they are done. Just look at how wiled up the crowd became after Robabeh's speech? Angry people* act crazy. They won't be able to control themselves. Something could happen to me. It won't be fair. I have a family to take care of. I promise to be quick."

Leans towards Jeff.

"Maybe my words will help calm this crowd down a little bit."

JEFF: *Seems to have been convinced.*

"I have no objections whatsoever. But I have to speak with these people using the broken Farsi that I know and try to persuade them. Otherwise control may be lost."

Jeff goes toward the crowd and begins to speak to them.

After a short while he turns to Arash and smiles.

"It took a while, but finally I made them understand what I was saying. Don't worry, they are convinced."

ARASH: *Looks up at the sky*

"Thank god almighty!"

He seems content.

JEFF: *Points to the crowd. They lift their blazing torches and form a circle around Jeff and Arash again. At Jeff's request they fetch a platform that looks like a step ladder. Jeff turns to Arash.*

"Mr Arash Vaziri, please climb up there and speak your heart out. Maybe you will be able to calm this crowd down a little bit. Otherwise, may god have mercy upon your soul tonight."

Arash takes out a bottle of water from inside his briefcase. Takes a couple of gulps. Takes a deep breath and climbs the stairs. The crowd is silent. Arash looks at the crowd and begins to speak calmly and deliberately.

ARASH: "My dear compatriots and complainants. I welcome you from the bottom of my heart. I thank each and every one of you for providing me with the pleasure of standing before you tonight in this sacred place that is a symbol of freedom of speech in the whole world. My dear plaintiffs, you have brought large amounts of trouble and hardship upon yourselves to *come here and freely express your complaints before Mr. Jeff Wilkinson, a representative of the British Department of Justice, complaining as to why I did not translate what you had to say in a way that you would be granted asylum."*

A commotion is heard from the crowd. They all seem to be objecting to what he has to say. Jeff tries to calm the crowd down.

"You have complained about me"

The crowd agrees with a loud yes.

"You consider me to be the root cause of all your misfortunes."

The crowd agrees with a loud yes.

"My dear fellow citizens! You fair people of Iran! I ask you before this

representative of the British Department of Justice, to pay good attention to what I have to say. The cause of all your troubles and hardships, your heartbreak and disappointments is the corrupt government and regime of the Islamic Republic who for decades has ruled the good people of Iran through lies, deceit and false pretences. This regime is the true enemy of the people. Four to five million Iranians have emigrated and dispersed around the world. Why have these people given up their homeland and dispersed around the world? Am I to blame for this destitution and misery?

"Our country is one of the richest in the world. Whatever is there that we want for in our own country that we should leave and beg like beggars in other countries of the world so that we are allowed to stay there and given some menial work? Tonight, before Mr. Jeff Wilkinson, I ask of you where has the wealth of our country gone? Whose corrupt pockets are being filled? Who is hoarding this wealth?"

Everyone is listening intently. The torches flames have somewhat subsided.

"You my dear suffering compatriots, my innocent fellow citizens, if we enjoyed political freedom and security in our homeland,"

"If we enjoyed financial security, a decent paying job, a comfortable

living which we incidentally well deserve would we ever bring this kind of humiliation upon ourselves? Who is responsible for all these crimes, all these betrayals?"

Says in a low voice

"Am I responsible for all this misery?"

He tries to diminish the crowd's fervour through a heart warming speech

The crowd is quiet and listening. The torches are slowly going down.

"Please go ahead and answer me as loud as you can, would we have left our dear country had we had the freedoms that are the basic rights of every human being so that we would need to apply for asylum and need the help of lawyers and interpreters to stay in these foreign countries. "

The crowd cry out No. Arash continues passionately.

"Why have you gathered at the speaker's corner tonight? Isn't it so that you can speak freely in this sacred place? Why shouldn't all of Iran be like this sacred place where everyone can freely express what they believe without fear of prosecution? Why shouldn't freedom of speech exist in our homeland?"

He continues angrily and emotionally.

"If someone dares to speak and criticizes the hellish situation in the country, they pour molten lead down his throat. They make life a living hell for him. They teach him a lesson that until the day that he dies he will never again dare to even think about protesting against or criticizing the government or regime. The prisons are overflowing with intellectuals. The murdering and plundering rulers of our country are committing unmentionable crimes and atrocities in the name of god and religion and they fear no god or man."

Arash's voice breaks, he takes a quick look at the crowd, he coughs slightly, the crowd becomes concerned. Jeff quickly hands him a bottle of water and a glass.

Arash pours himself some water. The crowd is anticipatingly waiting for him to resume. Arash drinks some water, clears his throat and continues.

"Where does it say in our holy book that young men and women may be raped and tortured to death? Who is responsible for all these crimes and unspeakable atrocities? Just look at this recent farce of an election that was recently held. They encouraged people to participate and vote for one of the four candidates that had made it through their illegal filters and system of elimination. They held debates and interviews on television. The moment they realized that the so called green opposition movement was victorious, they cheated and declared their own candidate a winner overnight and brutally and utterly oppressed the people's protest marches until blood flowed on the streets. They opened fire on people from the roof tops using live ammunition. Peaceful demonstrations were turned into a bloody massacre. They tortured writers and intellectuals and extracted false confessions under duress. My dear friends and compatriots! You must uproot injustice, brutality and corruption with the fire of your fury."

The crowd roars in consent.

"This corrupt government, to further humiliate our noble people, spent billions of dollars on shooting a few worms and frogs into space forty years after man walked on the moon just for propaganda purposes, and to appease their supporters."

"Will this so called scientific success put food on your table or bring you freedom or justice? Will it create jobs or improve your livelihoods? "

The crowd shouts a big No in unison.

"Will such shows bring you prosperity?"

The crowd begins to clap and applaud. The torch flames have now almost completely gone out. Arash wants to continue his speech when suddenly he notices Sassan and Nazanine amongst the crowd. They approach Arash's step ladder as they applaud. The crowd quietens down. Jeff approaches Sassan and Nazanine. They indicate that they want to climb the podium. Jeff approaches the podium and speaks with Arash.

JEFF: *"Please climb down, Mr Sassan Yazdani has obtained permission to speak."*

ARASH: *Jeff approaches the step ladder at Arash's gesture.*

"My speech isn't over yet. Furthermore, this couple's court case hasn't been decided yet."

JEFF: *He says it like he means it*

"I said get down, you have been up there giving a sermon for the past half hour. It is Mr. Yazdani's turn and of course Ms. Afshar's."

Arash gets down from the platform. He seems worried. Sassan climbs onto the podium as he holds a copy of Arash's commendation letter in his hand. The crowd is quiet. Sassan gives the crowd a look over and begins to speak.

SASSAN: *"My dear fellow asylum seekers, my dear compatriots who had to flee home and country with a world of hope and dreams in your hearts, and got yourselves and children here, having brought so many hardships upon yourselves."*

"Even risking your lives to get to this island of hopes and dreams. You know a hundred times better the troubles and suffering you have been through, much better than Mr. Arash Vaziri who has spent most of his life outside of his home country. Whatever he said, he had either read in some newspaper or seen on the internet. You felt this injustice and cruelty with your skin, flesh and bones. If it was any different, would you decide to abandon home and country and go into exile?"

The crowd agrees.

"If you see this deceitful trickster preaching to you about torture, injustice and unfair imprisonment it is to deviate your thoughts from the issues that count. This weasel who changes colours like a chameleon, was only earlier today defending this rotten and corrupt regime."

He points to Arash.

"This two-faced charlatan who is now criticizing the Islamic Republic, was singing the regime's praises only this morning and talking about the great eye popping developments and the progress the regime has brought to the people of Iran."

The torches flames gradually begin to brighten. Arash is worried.

"He was advertising the scientific achievements of the regime and talking about how they managed to shoot up some worms, frogs and cockroaches into orbit. He said that these achievements must not be taken lightly. He said that this regime must be praised and that Iran had gone far ahead under its governance. This is the rubbish he was trying to feed us. This coward stabbed all of you in the back."

"He didn't take a single step for you my dear compatriots in this foreign land so that you can obtain permanent residence and start a new life and not to have to worry about harassment by the fanatic militia and the regime's revolutionary guards anymore while you walk on the streets and go about your daily lives, not to worry about someone bothering you for the way you dress or how you fix your hair or even why you laughed? He never helped so that you won't any longer have to wake up in the dark of the night when the regimes agents break your door in and take your children to their dark and horrible dungeons and torture and rape them. A regime that even jails and tortures parents if they merely complain and enquire the fate of their children. You were hoping to live here without fear of that monstrous regime, to live in freedom as the English people do. But this louse didn't in the least help his fellow countrymen in this foreign land. He stabbed all of you in the back. This mean and unfeeling translator is the cause of your deportation and misery."

The torches are ablaze again. Arash is fearfully hiding behind Jeff and looking at the crowd.

"Arash Vaziri is the one responsible for all that went upon you after being deported from this country, this cronie is the one who caused it all. This person shamelessly distributed copies of a letter of commendation amongst you. The fool doesn't realise that this is actually a document that proves his betrayal of his compatriots. Just imagine, he actually expects us to thank and congratulate him for his service to the enemy!"

He shows a copy of the letter to the crowd.

"Just look at the bottom of this letter, all the Home Office barristers have signed it. They have all thanked Mr Arash Vaziri for his loyal service. Solicitors, whose only aim has always been to prove to the presiding

judge that your claims are all false and baseless. In fact, this bastard confirmed your deportation orders through the translations he did in the court of appeal. He actually helped the Home Office solicitors achieve their goals."

Nazanine *is standing next to Sassan. She points at Arash and in a very emotional voice.*

"Mr Vaziri, you are worried about the influx of refugees into this country, can you please tell the crowd"

Can one tell the little sparrow not to flee, not to go?

When the skilled hunter flies near and low

Can you ask the little bird to stay?

When it's nest and younglings may soon fall prey

Can you ask the nightingale not to fly?

It's free soul oppress and deny

Can you punish her for wanting to escape?

In whatever form, way or shape.

The iron cage the cruel jailer has built.

Must she stay and rot inside it and wilt?

The human soul too wants to be free

Free of oppression and suppression it wants to be

Can you ask a nightingale not to sing?

Shut it in a cage and clip it's tiny wings

Can you prevent a bird from nesting on the neighbour's tree?

Erect huge signs in the sky saying No entry

Can you place no entry signs in the sky?

And a birds entry into the neighbour's yard deny

Does a bird see borders from the sky when flying free and up high?

Come on tell them"

Arash is horrified. The torches are again ablaze and the crowd are holding them towards Arash.

Sassan continues.

"Seyyed Mohsen Razavi, this poor destitute soul who was thrown out of this country humiliated and deported, is amongst you tonight. Let's hear his story from his own mouth."

Seyyed Mohsen who is carrying a blazing torch walks towards the platform. Sassan and Nazanine quickly climb down. Mohsen steps on the podium. He wipes off his tears with his hand. The crowd has gone silent. Seyyed looks at Arash and sobs as he begins to speak.

SEYYED MOHSEN: *"The Home Office barrister asked me to name a few Friday prayer leaders and government ministers in the courtroom where Mr. Vaziri was translating. I was totally confused. I was dazed. I couldn't think properly. I begged him to help me. I asked him to name a couple of Friday prayer leaders or government ministers that he knew. But he wouldn't do it. I said, look man these people don't understand any Farsi."*

He takes a deep breath.

"If he mentioned a couple of these people's names that day in court, I would have been granted asylum and my life would not have turned into the hell that it has. I would not have been accused of being an apostate and an infidel and so violently tortured. They beat me so much in jail that I do not have a single unbroken bone in my whole body."

Seyyed Mohsen begins to sob loudly. The crowd rushes towards Arash. Arash picks up his briefcase and breaks through the crowd's circle. The crowd follow him while waving their blazing torches.

ARASH AND SARAH'S HOUSE

BEDROOM

Arash's face is covered with sweat. He is lying on the bed with his back to Sarah. He is mumbling something. Sarah has her hand on Arash's shoulder. She is shaking him. Arash wakes up. Takes a deep breath.

SARAH: *Turns to Arash as she turns the light on*

"You have been mumbling and talking gibberish in your sleep for over an hour now. You were talking in Farsi. It sounded as if you were having some kind of an argument with Jeff. I couldn't tell whether you were asleep or awake? I was worried for you."

ARASH: *As he gets off the bed*

"Sorry to have woken you up. I was having a nightmare. I have a terrible headache. I am going to the kitchen to take a couple of paracetamols, maybe I will feel better. I'll be back upstairs in a minute. Go back to sleep. Don't worry about me.

ARASH AND SARAH'S HOUSE

IN THE KITCHEN

Arash enters the kitchen and takes a couple of paracetamols out of the kitchen cabinet. He sits on one of the chairs at the small kitchen table and takes the pills with some water. He places the glass on the kitchen table and leaves the kitchen. He opens the door to the study and enters.

ARASH AND SARAH'S HOUSE

THE STUDY

The study is a small room with a small desk and a chair placed in the centre. A computer and a lamp are set on the table. A hand-made Persian carpet is spread on the floor. A bookcase stands next to the wall. A cabinet can be seen next to the bookcase. Arash opens the door to the cabinet, takes out a large cardboard box and places it on the desk. He looks at his commendation letter that is hanging in a frame. He notices an envelope containing a greeting card at the corner of the desk. The writing on the envelope says; 'To my dear father'. Arash opens the envelope and takes out the greeting card and reads it.

ARASH: *"I congratulate you for the commendation that you received. Congratulations from the bottom of my heart. I am proud of you. Love from Kian".*

Arash places the card back on the desk and delves deep into his thoughts.
ARASH: *"I have a terrible headache. I feel down. As if I have depression or something. What a strange dream."*

"It seemed so real. As if I was in a deep trance. Everything seemed so real to me. Even as we speak, when I close my eyes I could see those asylum seekers' angry faces. I am sure this nightmare stems from a subconscious conflict that is brewing deep within me. I feel that two opposing beliefs within my subconscious are pulling at each other. I must choose between them tonight. Make a firm decision. Otherwise these completely opposing forces will tear me apart. I will go completely mental. I feel as if I am at the cross roads. I must choose one of these two creeds and totally suppress and destroy the other, forever. What has put me in this predicament is doubts and indecision. No one is more responsible

for this than Sassan Yazdani and Nazanine Afshar. This couple managed to cause an upheaval in my psyche. I am not sure about anything any longer. But, tonight I must choose the path I will take. It's been many years since I hid and put away this box that is full of mementoes from my past, reminders of whom I used to be and where I come from, connecting me to my roots and essence. So that I could be true to my work, I chose to live in an area of London, where you do not find many Iranians, because I was always afraid of being obligated to do something that is in conflict with my commitments and work ethics."

"I always tried to deal with the issue impartially, just like a judge would. Under no circumstances was I ever influenced by these asylum seekers sobs and tears. Whatever they said, I translated verbatim. Even when just a yes or no answer could have changed the outcome and hence their destinies. I could have told them what sort of documents to present to the court and how to present their cases to be successful. I dare confess that I could have made it possible for the court to grant Rafat Shabani asylum had I slightly altered some of the things that he had to say in court. Had I not translated every contradicting statement that he made I could have prevented him from being deported from this country and sent to the gallows in Iran for his execution. The question is this, when it comes to a matter of life and death for a fellow countryman, what credence is there left for my work obligations?"

He takes a deep breath and continues.

"I feel that I was so deeply drowned inside my translating work and the ethical and legal obligations that it entails that I don't believe that even I could go back in time, I could still not translate Rafat's word any differently than I did at that time."

"At the same time, a guilty feeling takes over me whenever I think of this poor refugee. The nightmare I had tonight is the result of this ongoing conflict within my heart and soul."

Arash takes the letters out of the box. He puts them on the desk. He takes a bunch of photographs that have a rubber band around them out as well. He puts them on the desk and begins to stare at them. Sarah quietly opens the door to the study and enters. She looks at Arash for a few moments.

SARAH: *"What are you doing darling? I was worried about you. Why are you going through these at this time of night? Leave it till tomorrow. Come and rest for a while, you have to be in court first thing tomorrow."*

ARASH: *"I was looking at these pictures. Pictures of my childhood up to the time that I came to England. It's been 27-28 years since I last looked at these. I want to remind myself of who I am, where I come from and where my roots lie."*

SARAH: *"Well, couldn't you do this tomorrow? When you come back from work? There will always be time for looking at childhood pictures and old letters. But right now, what you need is rest. You really need it badly my dear."*

ARASH: *As he looks at some of the pictures*

"I think these pictures will be a great help in making me decide on what I am going to do tomorrow."

He points to a picture.

"This is the last family picture I ever took with my mother and father, God rest their souls."

He looks at the back of the picture.

"Thirty five years ago. That's a life time. Look at my father's face. Keyvan has taken after him. He would always say that he wished that I would go back home some day and help build my country. Alas, this dreaded revolution changed our destinies. Looking at these pictures, I am reminded that most of my relatives are either dead, migrated from Iran, killed in the eight year war with Iraq or are so displaced that I have no idea where they are. I am not in touch with any of them. Of course, some of them who held high positions when the Shah was in power, were captured and executed. You see this picture?"

He points to one of the photographs.

"This is my aunt Maliheh. After they executed her husband who was an officer in the army, she went crazy and died a couple of years later. She

205

wasn't that old, God rest her soul. These are my two uncles. I don't know whether they are dead or alive. I know that my cousins live in Canada and the United States. Should my uncles still be alive, they would be in their nineties since they were both older than my father. If you remember, last year when we went back to Iran we had to stay in a hotel like two foreign tourists."

"Instead of visiting with relatives, we went to museums and sightseeing and then returned to England. Not as if that place was the country of my birth. I remember that I felt like a foreigner and a stranger over there. Neither the people nor the places we saw seemed familiar to me. It was as if I was in some South American country."

SARAH: "My dear, life has it's many ups and downs. We are your family now. You are not alone. We are all you have now and we love you with all our hearts and souls. Forget the past. Think about us and the children. Not far from now the children will marry and have their own children. We will hold our grandchildren's hands and take them for walks in the park."

Arash smiles as he hears Sarah's words.

ARASH: "I think that Rosie will marry first. I am not too sure about Keyvan. For the time being he seems to be taking full advantage of his bachelorhood. He has had several girlfriends so far."

SARAH: "I guess this is part of his mental and physical development. Come on, you seem very tired. Your eyes look red."

Arash and Sarah leave the study and turn the light off behind them.

ARASH'S HOUSE

IN THE DINING ROOM – 8.00 am

Sarah, wearing casual clothes leaves the kitchen carrying a glass of orange juice. Kian, wearing jeans and a t-shirt is having breakfast. Sarah places the glass of orange juice in front of him.

KIAN: *"Thanks mum."*

SARAH: *Looks at the clock on the wall. Worriedly walks to the bottom of the staircase and shouts.*

"It is eight o'clock. Hurry. You must leave soon. You have to be in court first thing this morning."

ARASH: *Dashes down the stairs. Looks at his watch*

"Don't worry at all. There is plenty of time."

SARAH: *"Are you sure?"*

Pauses

"Then sit down and have some breakfast."

KIAN: *"Good morning dad. Did you see my card?"*

ARASH: *"Yes it was very nice. Thank you. Are you happy with your laptop? If not, I could change it for you."*

KIAN: *"No, that won't be at all necessary. It is exactly what I wanted. Thank you very much dad."*

SARAH: *Faces Arash*

"What would you like for breakfast?"

ARASH: *"I don't have an appetite yet. If I feel hungry before I go to court, I* *will drop into Yalda Café on the way. I will have a cup of tea and a sandwich before I go to work. Don't worry about me. You sit down and have a nice big breakfast, and don't forget to take your medicine. I*

had better go now."

Arash picks up his briefcase and walks toward the front door. Sarah follows him.

"Have a nice day Kian, take care."

He opens the front door. Walks out. Turns and kisses Sarah.

"Bye."

SARAH: *"I hope that you will have a great day. I pray for you my darling."*

ARASH: *With a smile "Thank you very much. See you soon. Goodbye."*

Sarah closes the door to the house and enters the living room. Kian continues to have his breakfast.

KIAN: *Turns to Sarah*

"Mum, was dad happy when you showed him his commendation letter last night?"

SARAH: *As she takes a box of cereal off the table,*

"Of course. This weekend your grandma, grandpa, uncle, aunt and their children are going to come over. We will have a party and celebrate. You know that Rosie and Keyvan will also be with us for the weekend."

KIAN: *"Mum"*

He pauses. Sarah is waiting to see what he has to say.

"Mum"

SARAH: *"Yes, go on, what is it?"*

KIAN: *"Dad seemed upset when he got home last night. This morning too, he seemed sick and pale. Is there anything wrong with dad?"*

SARAH: *Thinks for a while "No. I don't think so."*

"I don't think he is sick. God forbid."

She pauses a moment

"He couldn't sleep last night."

Kian takes his plate to the kitchen. Sarah looks at the clock on the wall. She turns to Kian.

"Go and change your clothes. You must go to college. You don't have much time left. I will clear the table."

Kian nods in agreement and climbs the stairs. What is going through Sarah's mind can be heard.

SARAH: *"I feel sick. I have a nasty headache. Last night not only he didn't sleep, but he didn't let me sleep either. He kept talking gibberish and mumbling in his sleep. It was hard to tell whether he was asleep or awake."*

She sighs

"I was really disappointed last night. I thought he would be a lot happier after seeing that commendation letter. All he did was give me a smile. I imagine anybody else would have jumped for joy. Lately every time he steps out the door and goes to work he looks like he is going to a funeral. He looks as if he is going to be tortured. God knows I am getting tired of this too. I can't take it any longer. If I were healthier, say maybe like ten twelve years ago, I would tell him to resign from this job and find something else to do. Wouldn't be important, like the time I managed the 'NEXT' store in Kensington. The salary and overtime I made then was more than what he brings in now. But what can I do? After that horrible surgery on my heart, I must thank God that I am still alive. They replaced most of my heart's arteries. Believe me, had the ambulance reached me two minutes later, I would have died right there in the middle of that 'NEXT' store. But it turned out O.K. The doctor tells me not to bring too much pressure upon myself. Rest, lie on the bed at least 10 minutes once every couple of hours. Relax he says! But how can I?"

"I am not complaining about my husband, God no, I fully understand how he needs to deal with a bunch of naive asylum seekers every day. It's a war of nerves. I cannot blame him. But what can one do? My dear, you are fifty five years old. In this economic crisis the likes of which even *granddad didn't experience, you have a well respected job dealing with judges and solicitors all day. Stop whining for god's sake. They say that next year unemployment numbers will pass three million. At least thank God you have a decent and respectful job. I told my loving and dear husband over one hundred times, once you leave the courtroom, just turn off your engine, shut everything off and stop thinking about work. Don't allow your work to take over your life. You eat, sleep and drink work."*

In the meantime Kian walks down the stairs.

KIAN*: As he walks toward the front door.*

"Bye mum."

WAITING AREA AT THE COURTHOUSE

9:00AM

Nazanine and Sassan are holding each other's hands and walking around the large room. They look at the people as they come and go. They seem indifferent to the events around them. They have stopped talking to each other as if they have run out of things to say. They aimlessly pace around the chamber. A few minutes go by. Suddenly Arash enters the room in a mad dash and attracts their attention. Arash hurriedly rushes around the room and talks to several court clerks as if looking for someone. They both look at him and follow him around the room inquisitively. He is loudly calling for someone in English. Jeff approaches him and tries to calm him down. They talk to each other and rush out into the corridor outside of Nazanine and Sassan's sight. Sassan looks at Nazanine.

NAZANINE:*"It appears as if something is going on. Why is he running around like a mad man?"*

Turns to Sassan

"What do you think has happened?"

SASSAN: *"I guess his guilty conscience eventually drove him mad. He wasn't acting like a normal person."*

NAZANINE: *"Not at all. It appeared as if he was looking for someone. He seemed very disturbed and upset."*

Sassan tries to look indifferent. They both walk toward a bench and sit down. They again notice Arash who is hurriedly walking toward the courtroom along with one of the solicitors. Time seems to have slowed down. They are both tired and impatient.

NAZANINE: *Turns to Sassan*

"What time is it?"

SASSAN: *"9:45am. I wonder what they are doing in that room?"*

NAZANINE: *"When one is anxious and worried time seems to slow down. It feels like we have been waiting here for hours. Nobody tells you anything. Why are there so many delays? This might not have anything to do with us."*

They both fall silent again. Jeff approaches them with a smile and indicates for them to follow him. They both enter the courtroom.

THE COURTROOM

SASSAN AND NAZANINE'S TRIAL

Sassan and Nazanine enter the courtroom and slightly bow in respect. The judge is sitting on his chair and the barristers and the other court staff have taken their respectable places. The judge looks at Arash. He quickly stands. The judge tells Arash to ask Nazanine and Sassan to stand up.

ARASH: *Turns to Sassan and Nazanine*

"Please stand up and face the judge."

Nazanine and Sassan stand immediately. The judge faces Sassan and Nazanine and begins to speak in clear and elaborate English for Arash to translate.

ARASH: *Turns to Nazanine and Sassan*

"The court has been presented with a document today that confirms what you have claimed is true. The judge, Mr. Peter Jones, has granted you asylum. You can now live wherever you want in this country. Unfortunately, you have been tried in absentia and found guilty of being 'corrupt on earth' back in Iran. An arrest warrant has been issued for you both. To protect your lives I suggest that you live in the apartment that we have provided for you under assumed names."

"All the rights and benefits of U.K. citizens now apply to you. You are under the protection of the laws of this country, I hope you can successfully adopt to the living conditions in this country. You have been through many hardships. Try and build a nice life for yourselves here. The necessary asylum documents will be presented to you. Welcome and good luck."

Arash who seems very emotional wipes a tear with a tissue and tries to control his emotions. Sassan and Nazanine look at one another in amazement and find it hard to believe what they just heard. The judge faces Arash and says something. Arash begins to translate while facing Sassan and Nazanine.

ARASH: *"The judge is asking if you have any questions?"*

SASSAN: *As if in a panic*

"Is our trial over? Doesn't the judge have any more questions for me?"

ARASH: *"No there is no longer a need to question you."*

Arash faces the judge

"No they do not have any more questions."

The judge brings down the gavel and declares the case concluded. Everyone stands as the judge leaves the courtroom. The solicitors come to Sassan and Nazanine, shake their hands and congratulate them. Arash translates for them. The Home Office barrister faces Sassan and Nazanine and says something to them in English. Arash won't translate what he said. The solicitor repeats what he said. There is a short pause. Sassan becomes a little worried. He turns to Arash and asks...

SASSAN: *"What is the Home Office fellow saying?"*

ARASH: *Seems embarrassed*

"He is saying that you should thank your interpreter, Mr Arash Vaziri, who just saved you from certain death."

Sassan and Nazanine thank Arash without fully understanding what was going on. They all leave the courtroom together. The barristers say goodbye to Arash, Sassan and Nazanine and leave.

ARASH: *"I will go with you to help you pack your things and move to an apartment in South London, your new home."*

NAZANINE: *She faces Arash in disbelief*

"Arash, does this mean that we are all done? Have they given us permission to stay? Or are we dreaming all this?"

ARASH: *Confirms*

"No you are not dreaming. The judge has granted you full asylum. There is nothing left for you to do here. I will give you my phone number. If there is anything you need, let me know."

JEFF: *Facing Arash*

"Friday morning, 9:30am, the Afghan refugee's name is Taher Maleki."

ARASH: *Turns to Jeff*

"Unfortunately I must inform you that you will need to hire a different translator for him."

He takes an envelope out of his pocket and hands it to Jeff.

"Please pass this along to the administration department."

Jeff takes the envelope and looks at it.

"This is my resignation ."

JEFF: *Looks shocked*

"Arash, you must be joking? Are you sure about this after all this time? It's not a hasty decision is it?"

ARASH: *He faces Jeff and says firmly*

"No, not at all. I will return to the courthouse at 4:00pm today to settle accounts. I would like to buy you a drink after you are done for the day."

JEFF: *"Look forward to it. I will be waiting for you."*

ARASH: *"See you later then."*

Jeff leaves the court. As Arash and Jeff were speaking in English,

Sassan and Nazanine were happily hugging each other. After a moment they notice that Arash is also leaving the courthouse. Sassan quickly catches up with him and they begin to speak as they leave the courthouse.

SASSAN: *"Excuse me Arash! May I ask how the court managed to come by those deciding documents? It appeared as if you provided them to the court? Where did you get them from?"*

Nazanine is listening intently, they are both facing Arash with a kind and appreciative look on their faces.

ARASH: *"The truth is that this morning I popped into an Iranian café to have breakfast."*

YALDA CAFÉ – LONDON

AROUND 8:00AM

Arash enters the café, a few men and women are having cake, tea, coffee and sandwiches. Most of them are Iranians. Arash stops in front of a rack of magazines and picks up an Iranian newspaper and walks to the counter. He begins to exchange the usual pleasantries with the owner who seems to know him well.

ARASH: *"Please let me have a coffee and a cheese sandwich."*

The shop owner places a coffee and a sandwich on the counter. Arash hands a ten pound note to the shop keeper and also shows him the paper. The shop keeper gives him the change. Arash picks up the coffee and sandwich and goes and sits at one of the tables. He begins to browse through the paper as he drinks his coffee. Suddenly he places his coffee back on the table, picks up the newspaper and holds it closer to him. His eyes almost pop out of his head in amazement. He reads an article on the second page. Then he lifts his head and closes his eyes for a moment. He takes a deep breath and opens his eyes, he stares at the newspaper.

A picture of Sassan and one of Nazanine have been published on the page next to one another. There is also a picture showing them together. Arash quickly reads the article one more time. He hurriedly goes to the shelf where the newspapers are kept and picks up a few more Iranian newspapers. He turns the pages and notices the same article and pictures in the other papers also. He grabs the papers, pays for them and dashes out of the café.

217

A LONDON STREET

AROUND 11:30AM

Arash, Sassan and Nazanine are walking along the pavement towards the bus stop. When they reach the bus stop Nazanine sits down on the bench. Sassan and Arash sit either side of her. Arash opens his briefcase and takes out two issues of different Iranian newspapers and shows each of them the relevant page. They both start reading. Whilst they are reading Arash takes out of his briefcase an envelope containing a photograph and hands it to Nazanine.

NAZANINE: *Glances at the photograph.*

"Oh look, this is my family photograph".

SASSAN: *Looks over curiously*

NAZANINE: *"Look, this is my mother Maliheh, that's my father Colonel Afshar, that's my mum's sister Aunt Mojdeh and her husband Babak and their son Arash, my cousin, and look, that's me, I must only be about 4. I've showed you similar family photos to this before haven't I".*

SASSAN: *Nods in agreement*

NAZANINE: *Looks at Arash with curiosity*

"Where did you get my family photograph from?"

ARASH: *Smiles and looks up,*

"Do you mean our family photograph?"

Both Sassan and Nazanine look at each other in shock

ARASH: *"It's a small world isn't it?"*

THE END

Lightning Source UK Ltd.
Milton Keynes UK
16 October 2010

161420UK00003B/11/P